Bragg's Truth

The Bragg Brothers #1

D.E. Haggerty

Molly's Misadventures

Chapter 1

I GLARE AT MY nemesis. You will not beat me. I refuse to be defeated by a piece of porcelain. Wait. Are toilets made of porcelain? Never mind. Bring it on, toilet.

I lift the lid off of the tank and gaze inside. This doesn't resemble the YouTube video I studied last night. At all. No matter. It's fine. I'll figure it out. I always do.

I grab my pliers and attempt to disconnect the tube thingy from the float thingy. Ugh! The tube thingy won't budge.

"Come on. Come on," I chant as I pull but there's still no movement. I inhale a deep breath and yank as hard as I can.

"Yes!" I shout as the tube finally moves. Only it doesn't disconnect. It breaks and water flies into my face.

"Stop!" I scream as I try to force the water back down into the tank with my hands.

Bang! Bang! Bang!

Thank the goddess up above. The handyman is here. I rush to the front door and whip it open. Hold on. This isn't my handyman. Not even close. This is Riley flipping Bragg. The person I want to see least of all in the world. Especially when I'm filthy from working on a toilet.

I snarl at him. "What are you doing here?"

Riley smirks as his gaze travels from my head to my toes. Yeah, yeah. I get it. I'm covered from top to bottom in toilet water while he looks amazing with his plaid shirt open to reveal all those delicious muscles.

No, not delicious. He's an asshole. Assholes aren't delicious no matter how much they resemble a cover model with their perfect smile and glorious hair. Thick brown hair I love to glide my hands through while he—

"I'm your new handyman," Riley announces.

He grins and his ocean blue eyes sparkle in amusement. I wonder how amused he'll be when I throw my pliers at him. Lucky for him I dropped them in my rush to answer the door.

"Where's Sirius?"

Sirius is my handyman. He's the handyman for everyone in Winter Falls, the small town in Colorado where I've lived my entire life except for when I attended culinary college.

I should have stayed at home.

Then, I wouldn't have ended up falling in love with a man over the course of one short week. The same man who then ghosted me after telling me he loved me. The very man who's now standing in front of me claiming to be my handyman. I don't think so.

Riley shoves his hands in his front pockets and rocks back on his heels. "He's retiring."

I gasp. Sirius is retiring? This can't be.

"Retiring? Since when?"

And how the hell didn't I know about this sooner? Sirius is supposed to be helping me with the renovations on the diner since my contractor up and quit on me. You tell a guy he made a mistake one time and he loses his mind. Although, if I'm being honest, it might have been the way I told him he screwed up. Oops.

"You can—" He cuts himself off. "Do you have a leak?"

"A leak? Where did you get such a crazy idea?" I motion to myself since I'm doing a hell of an impression of a drowned rat.

He ignores my sarcasm as he strides into the diner.

I chase after him. "Where are you going?"

"To fix your water leak."

"But you're not my handyman."

He stops at the door to the restroom and gestures to the water now flowing out of the room into the diner.

"Let's fix this problem first, shall we?"

"But…" The protest dies on my lips when he opens the door and I see the utter destruction in the restroom.

Oh no. I can't afford any more problems. I already spent more money on this renovation than I had budgeted. I knew the former owner, Gracious, hadn't updated any of the appliances in the kitchen since the 1960s, but I didn't realize she hadn't performed any maintenance on the place in just as long.

And to think I was beyond excited when she agreed to sell the restaurant to me. I thought it was the opportunity of a lifetime. Living in a small town, there aren't a whole lot of opportunities for a chef like me. Especially considering my determination to be my own boss.

Riley snags the pliers from the floor. "Get some towels for the water, will ya?"

I rush to follow his demand. I'm mopping up the floor with the towels before I realize how quickly I hurried to follow his orders. Damnit. This man should no longer have any power over me.

"Your toilet is fixed," he says from way too close behind me causing me to startle and drop the towels.

He grasps my shoulders and turns me around. "You okay, Moonbeam?"

I sway toward him before I remember. He's not mine. Not any longer. I push him away.

"The name is Moon. I'm not your moonbeam anymore, remember? You disappeared on me."

Pain flashes in his eyes. Blue eyes that remind me of the time we spent playing in the ocean in San Diego. "I'm sorry. Can you forgive me?"

Forgive him? Is he crazy? Does he think he can just waltz back into my life, snap his fingers and I'll forgive him? He's more likely to get another slap.

Confession time. I may have slapped Riley when he first showed up in Winter Falls. It wasn't my fault. He didn't reply to my calls and texts for three months. What did he think would happen when he showed up in town without a word of warning? Any woman would have slapped him.

I cross my arms over my chest and glare at him. "Why did you ghost me?"

His chin drops to his chest and silence fills the room.

"I should have slapped you harder," I mumble as I stomp toward the door and fling it open. "You should leave now."

"I'm not going anywhere. I'm your handyman." He scans the restaurant. "Judging by the state of things in here, you need me."

Who does he think he is? Reminding me of how badly I miscalculated when I began these renovations. And insinuating I can't manage without him. What a jerk.

"I don't need you," I hiss. I don't need a man. I don't need anyone. I've survived this long on my own. There's no reason to change a winning strategy.

"I meant you need a handyman."

I have YouTube and I know how to use it. Maybe the toilet repairs didn't work out great, but I can figure out how to tile and lay a floor from Google. I'm sure of it.

"You don't even live in Winter Falls," I point out.

"I do now."

He's got to be kidding. "What?"

"My brothers and I are all relocating to Winter Falls. We want to get to know Peace."

Peace is Riley's half-brother. It turns out Peace, a local boy I grew up with, has a whole family no one – including him – knew about. The man who raised Peace isn't his biological dad. His biological dad is Riley's dad.

I don't know all the details. I'm usually curious to learn all the gossip in town but heartbreak kind of took over my life for a while there. But no more. I'm done with pining over a man who can't bother to pick up a phone or answer a message.

Riley reaches for my hands. "And I want another chance with you."

I swat him away. "Second chance not granted."

He shrugs. "I'll wear you down."

If I could shoot lasers from my eyes, he'd be dead right now. Who does he think he is? My heart may still yearn for the man, but my head knows better. He has no staying power.

"In the meantime, you really do need a handyman. Don't sabotage the business you've dreamed of owning for your entire life because I'm an idiot."

Why did I share all of my hopes and dreams with him? Oh right, I fell in love with him and opened my heart to him. Lesson learned. I am hereby encasing my heart in a metal cage where it shall stay from now until the end of time.

"I'll give you a fifteen percent discount on my hourly rate."

Crap. I want to kick him out, but having help to finish the renovations of the diner would enable me to open earlier. The sooner I can open, the sooner I can start earning money to dig myself out of the hole I'm currently drowning in.

"Make it twenty and you have a deal."

"Deal." He holds out his hand.

When our hands touch, sparks explode and a shiver travels from my hand through my body until heat fills me. My body remembers exactly how well Riley can use his to make me see stars. How his strong arms can hold me in any position he wants while bringing me pleasure.

I cut those thoughts off and yank my hand away before I end up jumping into his arms and molding my lips to his. I will not give in to temptation. Project Forget How Sexy Riley Is, is hereby initiated.

"I'll expect you here tomorrow morning bright and early," I say as I shove him out of the diner and lock the door behind him.

He smirks at me from the sidewalk. I glare at him. He winks before strolling away while whistling.

I force myself to look away. I will not watch him walk away. I will not stare at his perfect ass. I won't. I will remain strong. He's a leaver, remember?

I've been left enough in my lifetime. No more.

Chapter 2

RILEY

I glare at my twin. "I'm literally standing right in front of you, Brody. Why are you texting me?"

And I'm not a chicken. He thinks I ghosted Moon because I'm afraid of a relationship. He's wrong, but I'm not enlightening him with all the reasons I was a total asshole. Those reasons are mute now anyway since I'm winning the woman of my dreams back. Plans are already in place.

Brody chuckles. "Reasons."

I groan. "Did you put another virus on my phone?"

As if on cue, music blares from my phone, and a video of some singer I recognize from the eighties starts playing.

"Gotcha!"

I don't understand how my twin can't manage to remember to wash his clothes, but he can somehow figure out how to send me malware via a gif.

I switch my phone off and shove it in my pocket. "Are we going inside or are we standing on the porch all night?"

I raise my hand to knock but drop it when I notice the rest of our brothers coming our way. There are five of us in total. Damon is the oldest. Elder and Miller are next. They're twins, too, although not identical like Brody and me. My twin and I are the babies of the family.

The door opens and Peace steps onto the porch. Oh wait. There are now six Bragg brothers. Peace is the half-brother we didn't know about until our dad was dying and he admitted to cheating on our mom when they were engaged.

Elder started a search to find out if Dad's 'indiscretion' had resulted in other Bragg siblings. And now we have a new half-brother, Peace.

"My mom is really nervous about meeting all of you. I know this whole situation has complicated written all over it, but can you go easy on her?" Peace asks.

Damon growls. "Do you need to ask?"

"I don't know you, so yeah, I need to ask."

"Can you believe our half-brother's name is Peace and he's an officer of the peace?" Elder teases.

Peace rolls his eyes. "I've never heard that joke before."

Miller stomps his feet. "Are you going to let us inside or are we going to stand out here freezing all night long?"

Peace frowns but waves us into the house. His parents are waiting for us in the entryway along with Peace's girlfriend, Olivia.

We stand around for a while staring at each other before Olivia speaks.

"I'm Olivia. Despite knowing better, I'm dating this cop."

Peace throws an arm around her shoulders. "You know you love me."

"Whatever you say, cop." She rolls her eyes. "Everyone already knows Miller and Elder since they've been living in Winter Falls while they stalked Peace."

No one corrects her since she isn't wrong. My older brothers relocated to this small town and founded the brewery, *Naked Falls Brewing*, all because they wanted to meet Peace. It took them several years to get up the nerve to speak to him, though, which sounds an awful lot like stalking.

Olivia points to me. "And I know you're Riley. It's hard to forget the man who got the hell slapped out of him at your party."

I lock down my muscles to stop myself from flinching. I can't blame Moon for slapping me. Not when I'm the one who screwed up. "I am."

"And you must be Brody since you're Riley's carbon copy."

Brody grins. "What's your phone number?" Peace growls. "What? I'm adding her to the family group app is all."

"Don't believe him," Damon says. "He'll send you gifs that cause your phone to bwak like a chicken for hours."

Olivia smiles. "You must be Damon, the oldest."

Damon scowls. "Not the oldest anymore." A big part of his personality is being the eldest brother, but now he has to reconcile himself to having an older sibling. He's not a happy camper.

Peace's mom steps forward. "I'm Clementine and this is my husband, Eagle. It's nice to meet all of you."

"You didn't seem happy to meet us when you were trying to stop us from establishing the brewery," Miller grumbles.

Pain flashes in her eyes. I lift my hand to shove Miller but Elder's already slapping his shoulder. "Knock it off. You promised to be civil."

"I am being civil," Miller grumbles.

I ignore him to reach forward and grasp Clementine's hand. "I apologize for him. He was dropped on his head as a baby." I kiss her hand and wink at her. She blushes and giggles.

Peace shoves me. "Stop flirting with my mom."

"I can't help it if I'm charming."

"I get why Moon fell head over heels for you," Olivia says.

At the mention of Moon's name, my body tightens. I thought I won the lottery the first time she looked at me with her big smile. Of course, she was laughing at me. I could not have cared less. Her brown eyes sparkled and I was hooked.

I miss her. I miss how she feels in my arms when she comes apart for me. I miss how she can barely tell a joke because she's laughing so hard you miss the punch line.

And I can't help but admire her determination. But it's my turn to be determined now. I will win her back. I don't care what I have to do to prove to her I'm serious, I'm all in.

"Moon's the one who slapped him?" Brody asks.

I elbow him. He knows damn well who slapped me. "None of your business."

He smirks. "Obviously, I'll be the best man at the wedding."

"Not hardly."

"You going to live in sin?"

"I think I like this brother," Olivia says.

Peace groans. "You just like the idea of living in sin."

She grins. "You know it."

"Someone likes me more than you," Brody teases me.

I wrap my arm around his neck and put him in a headlock. Eagle pushes between us and shoves us apart.

"Shall we sit down?" he asks while Brody and I growl at each other. When no one moves, he grumbles, "It wasn't a suggestion." And everyone hurries to the living room.

"Are you going to come and cook for us at the brewery since the diner's closed now?" Elder asks Eagle as everyone settles in the living room.

"The diner isn't closed. It's being renovated," I correct him.

He rubs his hands together. "This is going to be fun."

I frown. There's nothing fun about the mess the diner's in. I didn't see much before Moon kicked me out but the pipes are definitely old and need replacing.

"Go ahead," Eagle nudges Clementine.

"I need to apologize." She wrings her hands. "I didn't realize your father was engaged. I never would have … I mean to say …"

Eagle kisses her forehead. "Stop, Emmy. It's not your fault."

Elder clears his throat. "Mrs. Sky."

"Clementine. Call me Clementine."

"We don't blame you," Elder is quick to reassure.

I'm surprised when Miller grunts in agreement. Miller is the Bragg brother who resists change the most. I still can't believe he agreed to Elder's plan of moving to Winter Falls and founding a brewery to be near our half-brother, Peace. But wherever Elder goes, Miller tends to follow.

Clementine stares at us for a long moment before nodding. "Anyway, I understand all of you will be living in Winter Falls and I'm hoping we can have a relationship."

Olivia groans.

"What's wrong?" her boyfriend asks.

"I grew up with one brother. He was the definition of over-protective. Does this mean I now have five more overprotective brothers to handle?"

"Considering how much trouble you managed to get into growing up, I don't think Beckett was very protective."

Olivia flutters her eyelashes up at him. "Or maybe I excel at getting my way."

"You're much too pretty to be a sister of us Neanderthals," I say with a wink.

She wags her finger at me. "You're trouble."

Not anymore. I'm now a one-woman man. Or I will be. As soon as I can convince my one woman she's mine. Good thing I enjoy a challenge.

"The whole lot of them are trouble," Damon complains.

"And you aren't? Do you not remember the time you 'borrowed' Dad's car without permission to impress the girl you were dating?" Elder starts.

"Tiffany. You took her to prom. And Dad was pissed," Miller continues.

"Especially when he found her underwear in the backseat," Elder finishes.

Damon smirks. "It wasn't Tiffany's underwear."

"You dawg."

I frown. Damon isn't the only slut in the Bragg family. Our dad didn't understand what the word faithful meant. His indiscretions didn't stop with Peace's mom.

I thought he was the coolest dad in the world until I caught him sneaking in when I was in high school. But since I was sneaking home at the same time, I couldn't exactly tattle on him without getting into trouble myself.

Olivia's nose wrinkles. "I don't get it. How do you accidentally forget your panties? Do you go commando? Yuck."

Damon wiggles his eyebrows. "The last thing a girl is thinking about after I—"

Clementine claps her hands to cut him off. "It's decided. I'm adopting all of you for as long as you live in Winter Falls. I expect you here every Wednesday night for dinner." Her gaze locks on mine. "With your partner."

I wink. "I wouldn't want to cheat on you, my Clementine."

She giggles. "Olivia's right. You are trouble."

Olivia pumps her fist. "Awesome. I got my first nod of approval from the mother-in-law."

Clementine freezes. "If you two elope, I will never forgive you."

Peace raises his hands in surrender while his girlfriend backpedals. "It's a saying. Nothing more. We're not married. We're not engaged. We're not even living together."

"I expect you to get married before you give me grandchildren." She wags her finger at me and my brothers. "That goes for all of you."

Brody raises his hands in surrender. "I always wrap before I tap."

"Cover your stump before you hump," Elder adds.

"Don't be silly, wrap your willy."

"No glove. No love."

"Don't be a fool, wrap your tool."

Olivia dissolves in giggles. "Are you certain Elder and Brody aren't the twins?"

Elder puffs out his chest. "I'm two years older. I remember wiping this one's ass." He thumbs his finger toward Brody.

"You didn't wipe my ass when you were two years old," Brody protests.

"Maybe not but I changed all of your diapers," Damon says.

"You did not," Miller grumbles.

Eagle wraps an arm around his wife and kisses her temple. "You always wanted a big family."

Clementine smiles. I guess she's not bothered by the sex talk. Good to know since it gets a lot raunchier than this.

Moving to Winter Falls might be the best decision of my life. I gained a new brother. The rest of my brothers are growing closer. And, if I have it my way, the love of my life will be sitting next to me on this sofa for family dinners soon.

Make no mistake about it, I will have it my way.

Chapter 3

I GROAN FROM WHERE I'm laying on my sofa when someone pounds on the door. After spending the entire day doing manual labor to get the diner ready to open, I lack the energy to roll onto my back. Standing to answer the door is not happening. Plus, I have zero interest in talking to Mr. Sexy Handyman.

"Open up or I'm coming in," Ashlyn shouts.

Crap. If I have zero interest in talking to Mr. Sexy Handyman, I have minus zero interest in talking to my best friend. The best friend who doesn't know about my past relationship with Riley, which is considered a best friend violation in Ashlyn's books. And she takes those books very seriously.

"Five. Four. Three. Two."

I groan and roll to my feet at the same moment Ashlyn barges into my house.

"It's alive!"

I lay back down on my sofa. "Barely."

She frowns. "What's wrong with you? Are you sick?" She makes a cross with her fingers in the air and backs away.

Oh how I wish I could lie to my best friend and claim I have some horrible communicable disease, but I've known her since kindergarten; she can spot me lying from a state away. Unfortunately, I'm speaking from experience.

"I'm not sick. I'm exhausted."

"Exhausted from playing hide the sausage?"

"I'm not playing hide the sausage with anyone."

"But you did play hide the sausage with Riley."

"Can we stop saying hide the sausage now?"

"And you didn't tell me about it." She pouts.

"Way to make this all about you."

She grins. "Hello! Have you met me? Everything's about me."

She's not wrong. Ashlyn prefers to think of herself as the star of everyone's life. And I'm her trusty sidekick.

"Can you come back and do your song and dance performance another day?"

"Uh oh. Snarky Moon has arrived at the party. What's wrong?"

"I told you. I'm exhausted."

"Dude—"

"I'm not a dude and this isn't a nineties comedy."

She ignores me. This happens a lot.

"Exhausted isn't an excuse. I'm a mother, I manage a recording studio, and I'm a famous audiobook narrator."

I slow clap. "Good job. Ashlyn Bashlyn is wonder woman. You can do it all."

She bows. "I know. Thank you."

"Can you please exit stage door left now? I have less than eight hours before I have to be back at the diner."

She shoves my feet off of the sofa and sits next to me.

"Oh, moon pie. How silly are you? Do you seriously think I'm going to leave before I get all the nitty, gritty details of the 'Moon and Riley show'?"

"There are no nitty, gritty details."

She giggles. "You slapped him. Like. Bam! Who's your mama? There are many, many details. And I want all of them."

I bury my face in my hands. I had to slap Riley in front of the entire town? I couldn't have slapped him in private? Or, and this is a novel idea, not slapped him at all?

Ashlyn rubs circles over my back. "What did he do? Did he hurt you? Did he physically abuse you? Emotionally abuse you? I will cut a man."

She starts shadowboxing. Or, at least, I think that's what she's doing. The way her arms are flailing around, she's more likely to hurt herself than anyone else.

"Stop! He didn't abuse me."

"Alrighty then. Scenario number one has been eliminated."

"Did you make a list of possible scenarios?"

She taps her forehead. "They're all up in here."

Which means yes, she made a list.

"And, since scenario number one is not applicable, you have no excuse for keeping your bestie in the dark."

"I don't feel like talking about it."

She grins. "Okay. We'll drink instead." She pulls a bottle of tequila out of her bag.

"I can't do shots of tequila. I need to work tomorrow."

"And I'm a mother who has to care for her child tomorrow. And, yet, here I am."

She hands me a shot glass and pours some tequila into it. I notice she doesn't pour herself a drink. I narrow my eyes on her.

"How do I know you didn't put poison in my drink?"

She smirks. "You don't."

I know better than to drink this. The last thing I need is a repeat of the whole syrup of ipecac incident. Talk about a shit show. Literally. I slam the shot glass on the coffee table.

Ashlyn shrugs. "Well, it was worth a try."

"Can you give me this? I know it's impossible for people in Winter Falls to understand the concept of privacy, but can't you give me some privacy this one time?"

"One." She holds up her index finger. "I gave you privacy for months."

I snort. Privacy my ass. She begged and cajoled me the entire time.

"Two. I'm not just any old resident of Winter Falls. I'm your best friend."

Too bad I don't have a time machine. I could go back to the day in kindergarten when I showed her the error of her ways. I wouldn't have warned her about putting a Lego up her nose. I'd let her suffer instead.

"Three. How can I keep the gossip gals off your back if I don't know what's happening?"

She's crazy if she thinks she can keep the gossip gals off my back. No one has that kind of power.

The gossip gals are five elderly members of the community who think it's their duty and obligation to stick their noses in everyone else's business. They're actually proud of their designation as gossip gals. Seriously. They have t-shirts made for special occasions.

"The gossip gals are uncontrollable."

"I know. Aren't they awesome? I want to be them when I grow up."

Usually, I agree with her. They are awesome. Except. In addition to being busybodies, they also fancy themselves matchmakers. And I'm afraid they currently have their sights set on me. They can keep on looking for a target because this girl is no one's target.

"Come on, moon pie." Ashlyn sticks out her bottom lip and pouts. "Tell me what happened."

I groan. I know I'm going to have to come clean sometime, I guess it might as well be now. Maybe she'll give me some peace once I bare my soul to her. And maybe the gossip gals will move out of Winter Falls. In other words, not happening.

"Fine. I'll tell you."

She cheers and claps, but I poke her.

"There will be no interrupting."

She feigns zipping her lips.

"I met Riley when I was in San Diego for the cooking course I took a few months ago."

"Which is when you took a trip to pound town."

"I thought your lips were zipped."

She zips them back up again.

"We had a wonderful week together. I told him all my hopes and dreams. We discussed the idea of me moving to California."

She gasps.

"No interruptions."

She raises her hand as if to ask permission.

"No!"

She drops her hand with a pout of her lips.

"It was perfect. I thought he was perfect. But when I returned to Winter Falls, he ghosted me."

"No way!"

"Yes, way. So, when I saw him at Olivia's party at the yoga studio, I kind of lost my mind."

"And now he's your handyman," she says, proving the rumor mill is alive and well in Winter Falls even when you ignore it.

"He claims Sirius wants to retire."

"It's true. Clove says he needs to slow down."

Clove is his wife and a member of the gossip gal gang. She also owns the coffee shop in town, *Clove's Coffee Corner.* When she first found out I wanted to be a chef, she offered me a job. But I've always dreamed of being my own boss and turned her down.

Probably not my smartest move since there's entirely too much competition in the food business in this town of barely over one-thousand inhabitants. There's a bakery, a café, a restaurant at the brewery, and the diner. I knew I couldn't start a new endeavor, which is why I jumped at the chance to take over the diner.

But, once again, I leaped before I looked. I should have done an inspection of the diner before I agreed on a price with Gracious. But I didn't and now I'm stuck with a huge loan for the business as well as the cost for the renovations I didn't anticipate.

"Riley agreed to a twenty percent discount."

"I bet if you threw a little no pants dance in there, he'd lower his wages more."

"I'm not going to sleep with the man who broke my heart to get a discount. I have some morals!"

Not many, mind you. But some, for sure.

"Broke your heart! You love him. You want to marry him. You want to make babies with him."

I slap her shoulder. "Knock it off. I'm not you. I don't need to get knocked up the second the man I've been pining after for years gives me the green light."

She waggles her eyebrows. "Oh honey, he gave me more than the green light."

"I never should have helped the gossip gals remove the bed from the spare bedroom."

"Ha! I knew you helped."

She whips out her phone.

"What are you doing? You can't tell Rowan."

She rolls her eyes. "I'm not telling Rowan about the bed. The whole one bed situation worked out entirely too well for me. No, I need to tell him I won't be home tonight."

"Are you going out carousing?"

"Don't be silly, moon pie. I'm getting drunk with my best friend while she cries on my shoulder about the asshole who ghosted her. Afterwards, we're making plans to prank his ass. I have plenty of syrup of ipecac left. And I know you have a ton of glitter."

This is why she's my best friend. She may be crazy and drive me nuts ninety-nine percent of the time, but she's always there when I need her. Not like the man whose name shall no longer be mentioned.

Chapter 4

RILEY

"Wow!" I say as I look around Main Street. "Winter Falls goes all out for Christmas."

"This isn't a Christmas festival," Peace corrects.

It sure looks like Christmas. "What is it, then?"

"It's Yule."

I scratch my beard. "Aren't Yule and Christmas the same thing?"

"Yule is a Pagan tradition to celebrate the sun beginning its return to us."

"The celebration has the same appearance as Christmas, though." I indicate the mistletoe and ivy decorations.

Peace laughs. "You've got a lot to learn about Winter Falls."

Winter Falls is unlike any place I've ever been to before. Any small town was bound to be a shock since I grew up in San Diego and lived there my entire life, but I'm pretty sure most towns don't host Pagan festivals.

Someone zips by on a golf cart. "What's the deal with those?"

There are golf carts everywhere in town but when I asked someone where the golf course was, I got a thirty-minute extremely detailed lecture on how golf courses are ruining the Earth.

"Winter Falls is the first carbon neutral town in the world," he says as if that explains everything.

"And?" I prod.

"Cars, except for electric ones, are banned from the town."

My brow furrows. "But I have a truck."

"You were given an exemption because of your handyman business. You can't exactly load up wood and all your supplies in a golf cart."

"There are a lot of rules to learn living in this town."

"Only about the environment. The rest," Peace smirks, "is pretty much live and let live."

I cock an eyebrow. "Really? I could race around naked and no one would care?"

"You obviously haven't met Forest yet."

"I know what a forest is."

He chuckles. "Not a thing. A person."

Does he mean a person named Forest? "Winter Falls is con-fusing."

"You'll get used to it. Assuming you're staying."

I spot a glimpse of long blonde hair I know feels like silk in my fingers amongst the crowd. *Moon.* "I'm staying."

Peace grins when he notices where I'm looking. "Good luck," he says and saunters off.

I mumble my goodbye since all of my attention is focused on getting to Moon. Although we've technically been working at the same location for the past few days, I haven't seen much of her. While I've been repairing the bathrooms at the diner, she's been working in the kitchen.

Whenever I took a coffee break, she disappeared into her office with a slam of the door. I got the 'leave me alone' message loud and clear.

I step in front of her to block her path. "Moon."

"Riley." She nods and attempts to skirt around me. Not happening.

"I brought you a present." I hold the wrapped package out to her.

She scowls as she retreats a step. "You can't buy me."

"I'm not trying to buy you."

"Then, why did you *buy me* a gift?"

"Because I want to spoil you."

"Spoil me?"

"Yeah, you know, treat you well. Show you how special you are to me."

"Special?" She snorts. "Was I special to you when you were ignoring my phone calls and not texting me back?"

"Damnit, Moonbeam. I said I messed up. Won't you forgive me?"

"Sure."

The tension in my shoulder releases. She's forgiving me. I smile and reach for her, but she dances away from me.

"As soon as you tell me why you ghosted me. And it better be good, handyman."

Before I have a chance to figure out how to get away with not telling Moon the truth without lying to her, an elderly woman next to Moon claps. "This is wonderful."

Moon rolls her eyes to the sky as she mumbles, "I knew this would happen."

I wink at the woman. "I don't believe we've had the pleasure of meeting."

"Oh, he's a charmer."

"Bet he can charm the pants right off of Moon," another elderly woman says as she joins us. "We'll call this one Project Do Over."

For some reason, her words cause Moon to lose her mind. Her hands fist as she shouts, "No! No projects! No bets! Nothing! You hear me, Feather? Nothing!"

Another woman raises her hand. "What about me? Can I bet? I'm betting on the charmer."

A muscle ticks in Moon's jaw and her nostrils flare. "Of course, you are. No one in this town ever takes my side."

"I'm on your side," I tell her.

She narrows her eyes on me. "You don't count."

"Why don't you introduce me to these lovely women?" I ask instead of telling her how much I plan to count in her future.

"This is Feather, Petal, Sage, Cayenne, and Clove." She points to each woman in turn. "Collectively, they're known as the gossip gals."

"It's not nice to call someone a gossip."

"We actually prefer the term busy body," Clove says.

"But gossip gal has a nice ring to it, don't you think?" Sage asks.

Cayenne elbows her. "Let's show him our sweatshirts."

"One, two, three," Sage counts down before they open their jackets and reveal bright pink sweatshirts with the words *Yule Love The Gossip Gals* printed on them in sparkly gold.

I chuckle. "Those sweatshirts are adorable. Did you make them yourselves?"

"I made them," Petal says. "I'm the artistic one."

"It's lovely to meet you, Petal." I kiss her cheek.

"Isn't it lovely to meet me, too?" Feather asks and taps her cheek.

"Of course." I kiss her cheek, too. "Who else needs a kiss?"

Sage elbows her way to the front of the group. "I'm the leader. You should give me two kisses."

Out of the corner of my eye, I notice Moon trying to sneak off. Not on my watch.

"I'm sorry, ladies. I owe you a rain check," I say before chasing after Moon. I catch her when she's nearly at the diner.

"Nuh-uh." I grasp her hand and pull her away. "No working today. You need a day of rest."

She yanks out of my hold. "How do you know what I need? You don't know me."

I crowd her until she's flattened against the building. "I know you, Moonbeam."

"Stop calling me, Moonbeam," she growls.

I tuck a strand of her hair behind her ear and her eyes fall closed as a shiver works its way through her body.

"But you are my moonbeam."

"I'm not your anything," she claims, but her words come out breathy. She's as affected by me as I am by her. But she's fighting it. I decide to give her a reprieve.

"Do you want your present now?"

"I told you. You can't buy me."

I ignore her – I'm never going to win this argument – and hand her the wrapped gift. I step away for her to open it.

"We don't do gifts in Winter Falls," she says as she stares at the package.

"What are all the presents doing laying around the town square if you don't do gifts?"

She rolls her eyes. "Those are little surprises. Everyone in town and all the tourists bring one wrapped gift. The idea is to bring something that has brought you joy in the past but you no longer use. Once you've contributed a gift, you can choose a surprise gift."

"What about presents from friends and family?"

She glances away. "I don't know what families do."

This right here is exactly why she's getting a gift from me. Her parents are jerks. They left on a road trip when she was sixteen and never returned. They called and told her since she was now old enough to be responsible for herself, they were going to do some traveling.

"Do your parents come home for the Christmas holidays?" I ask, although I'm afraid I already know the answer.

She shakes her head.

I swallow my growl. She needs my support, not my anger. "When do they come home?"

She shrugs.

I swear underneath my breath. My dad was a serial cheater but at least he was there for us kids. Unless he was traveling for work, he showed up at every football game, every birthday, and every holiday.

"Have they contacted you recently?"

"No," she whispers.

I frame her face with my hands. "If they don't want to spend time with you, they're the idiots. It doesn't reflect on you."

Tears well in her eyes and she opens her mouth. Finally. I'm getting through to her. But she clears her throat and pushes me away. "I don't want to discuss this. And, if I did, I certainly wouldn't want to discuss it with you."

"Will you at least open your present?"

Her nose wrinkles as she studies the gift-wrapped package in her hands.

"Will you tell me why you ghosted me?" She holds up a hand before I have a chance to come up with an excuse for not answering. "Never mind. If you don't want to tell me, I don't want to know."

She presses the present into my hands. "Goodbye, Riley Bragg."

I don't say goodbye. Because this isn't the end. No way. No how. Seeing the pain in Moon's brown eyes has served to reinforce what I already thought before, she's mine. She's mine to take care of. She's mine to cherish. I'm not letting her push me away.

Chapter 5

I STARE AT THE kitchen in the diner. I thought I could keep some of the appliances, do a bit of deep cleaning, and – boom! – I'd be ready to open. I wish.

The appliances aren't up to code. Which is totally fine when you have an existing business. Not so much when you're renovating and plan to open a new business. Unfortunately, even businesses in Winter Falls have to follow health and safety code regulations.

"Hello!"

I groan and bury my face in my hands. Riley. I was hoping he wouldn't show after I refused to accept his gift yesterday. I can't believe I nearly kissed him. I know I'm the queen of act first, think never, but I should know better with Riley. He broke my heart once. I'm not giving him a chance to break it again.

I yank the door open. "What do you want?"

"World peace. Oh wait. We're in Winter Falls. I think I'm supposed to say a healthy planet?"

I sigh. "What are you doing here?"

He shakes his hips to draw my attention to his toolbelt. "I'm here to work."

"Shake it, baby. Shake it!" Clove shouts from across the street.

"He can shake those hips for me anytime!" Feather adds from her spot in front of her ice cream shop, *Feather's Frozen Delights.*

I grab Riley's arm and drag him inside the diner.

"No need to hurry, Moonbeam," Riley rumbles in his deep voice. I shiver at the memory those words bring up. We were laying in bed and I was—

"Don't be mean, Moon," Clove shouts and brings me back to the present.

I glare at her as I shut the door behind us. "Those women will eat you alive if you let them."

Riley waggles his eyebrows. "I'd rather leave the eating to you."

I slap him. "Can't you be serious for one minute?"

He crosses his arms over his chest and his long-sleeve t-shirt strains to contain his muscles. Muscles I know for a fact are covered in smooth tanned skin. Skin that tastes like the sun and sea.

"You need to chill out," he says, and thoughts of how good his skin tastes fly out of my head.

"Me?" I pound my chest. "I need to chill out? And how do you suggest I manage that? I have a mountain of debt and no way to earn money because this place needs a ton more work than I could have ever imagined. My contractor quit. My regular handyman wants to retire to go on yoga retreats with his wife.

And my new handyman would rather flirt with old ladies than work."

I'm gasping for breath by the time I finish my tirade. Riley folds me into his arms.

"It's okay. Everything will be okay," he murmurs as he rubs his hand up and down my back.

"You don't get it. Everything is riding on this. If I can't make the diner work, I'll be bankrupt *and* I'll have to leave my home."

He grasps my chin and bends down to meet my eyes. "You're not going bankrupt and you're not leaving Winter Falls."

"Easy for you to say. You're made of money."

"I am?" He pats his stomach. "Feels like skin and bones to me. You want to touch for yourself to check?"

I bite my bottom lip. Touch those six-pack abs? I'm not an idiot. Yeah, I want to touch them. I reach toward him. My hand is nearly on his body when I realize what I'm doing. Falling into his trap again.

"Are you some kind of magician?"

"Are you saying I have a magic wand?" He punches his hips.

I roll my eyes so hard I'm surprised they don't get stuck. "You're a goofball."

"Correction. I'm a charming goofball."

"Whatever. Are you going to work sometime today or are you going to strut around like a peacock all day long? I'm not paying you for your looks."

He feigns flipping his hair. "The looks are free."

There's no talking to this guy. I whirl around and stomp toward the kitchen.

"What needs to happen in here?" Riley asks as he follows me.

"We have to gut the kitchen. Then, we have to put in a new backsplash, lay a new floor, and install new appliances."

He places his hands on his hips as he studies the room. "Have you bought the supplies yet?"

"Not yet. I, ah..." I cut myself off. I think we've had enough of me blurting out my money woes for one day. The last thing I want is for Riley to feel sorry for me. Pity is for losers.

"I get a discount at the big box store in White Bridge," Riley says, and my ears perk up. "I can pick up the tiles for the backsplash and the floor, as well as the other supplies after we're finished here."

"What kind of discount?" *Please be one-hundred percent. Please be one-hundred percent.*

"Thirty percent."

Maybe a hundred percent was a bit unrealistic.

"Okay. I have everything picked out already. I can give you my sketches," I say before he can ask me to accompany him to White Bridge.

A thirty-minute drive alone with him in his truck is more temptation than this woman can handle. Especially if he begins a charm offensive. He's entirely too charming for his own good.

"Great." He rubs his hands together. "Let's get to work."

"Can I use the sledgehammer?" He waggles his eyebrows and his mouth opens, but I slap a hand over his mouth before he can speak. "Nope. No lame jokes about your hammer and how I can use it."

He winks. "But you can," he mumbles from beneath my hand.

I give up. I seriously give up. You can take the man out of charm school, but you can't take the charm out of the man.

It's not long before we fall into a good rhythm. I break stuff up and Riley carries everything outside to be sorted and recycled.

"Make sure you put the broken tiles in a separate container," I yell after him.

He pauses. "Is this some weird Winter Falls thing?"

"Nope. My friend, Soleil, is an artist. She wants to try her hand at 'mixed media art'. Whatever that means."

"Soleil? Is she the one who knits vibrator covers?"

Damn him. How am I supposed to get over him when he remembers every single thing I told him during our week together? Most men forget what you say the second it comes out of your mouth. But not Riley. His mind is apparently a sponge.

"Yep," I say and return to breaking stuff.

Who knew breaking stuff is therapeutic? My arms and shoulders are aching but my worry about money and the future disappears as I continue to pound the sledgehammer at the countertops and cupboards and tiles.

No matter how good it feels, there's a limit to how much I can do before my muscles scream for a break. I set the sledgehammer down and slide the safety glasses into my hair. I remove my gloves and stuff them in my back pocket.

"Can you grab me the last tile?" Riley asks.

I don't think to put on my gloves before I pick up the tile. "Ow," I say as the ragged edge cuts into my hand. I drop the tile and it breaks into a million pieces on the floor. I groan. Great. More work.

Riley rushes to me. "Are you okay? Let me see."

I wave him away. "It's fine. It's barely a scratch." I lift my hand to show him but there's now blood dripping down my arm. I sway at the sight.

He catches me and lifts me into his arms. "Where's your first aid kit?"

"My office."

He carries me to the room.

"You do realize my hand is cut and not my legs?"

"Let me take care of you," he insists.

I should refuse, but no one's taken care of me since I was sixteen years old and my parents took off on their 'travels'. And I can admit – if only to myself – how good it feels for someone to care enough to want to help me.

Riley places me in my office chair with entirely too much gentleness. I scowl to hide how much I'm enjoying him caring for me. "I'm not made of spun glass."

He ignores my comment. "Where's your first aid kit?"

I point to the top of the cabinet and he grabs the kit before kneeling in front of me.

"It's a nasty cut, but I don't think you need stitches," he says as he studies my hand.

"Good. Stitches would slow me down."

"I hope you don't think you're going to continue to help with the renovations with this cut."

"Watch me."

He frowns as he removes some antiseptic wipes from the kit. "This is going to hurt."

"Do your worst, handyman. This is not my first injury. Not even close."

When your best friend is Ashlyn, it's hard to escape injury while growing up. We actually have a running count of how many stitches we've each had. She's lucky I don't have time for a hospital visit or I'd take the lead.

He gently wipes away the blood and cleans the wound. "I think the bleeding's stopped."

He leans close and blows on my skin. Damn. It feels good to have his breath on my skin. I bite my lip before I moan.

"Great." My voice comes out all breathy. Having Riley kneeling in front of me is doing strange things to my body. Things I normally enjoy. Like tingling all over. Heat in my belly. Warmth in my core.

He throws the wipes on the ground before digging a bandage out of the kit and putting it on the cut. "All done." He pauses. "Except this."

He stares into my eyes as he leans over and kisses the bandage. And I melt. It's a good thing I'm sitting because my legs have turned to jelly.

My telephone buzzes in my pocket and I nearly jump out of the chair at the distraction.

"Saved by the bell." Riley winks before standing and sauntering out of my office.

And I don't watch his ass as he walks. Nope. Not me. I'm done with Riley, remember?

Chapter 6

"THE TIME HAS COME!" Ashlyn announces when I open my front door to find her standing on my porch.

I scan her outfit. "Time for what? For us to go diving for lost treasure in the Pacific?"

Her eyes light up and she bounces on her toes. "Do you know about lost treasure in the Pacific Ocean? Have you been holding out on me? Do you have a map? A map is essential."

Her excitement at the idea of a treasure hunt isn't surprising. Ashlyn and her sisters found some buried money from a bank heist committed in the last century buried outside of town a while back and now my best friend thinks she's an expert treasure hunter.

I'm still pissed I wasn't allowed to join the search, but she says it was 'sister bonding' time. Since I don't have any siblings, I couldn't argue with her, although I was disappointed. And, okay, it hurt to be excluded. But I will never admit to being hurt out loud.

"No, crazy woman. I'm not going on a treasure hunt. I don't have a map."

Her nose wrinkles. "Then, why are we standing here discussing lost treasure?"

I indicate her outfit. "Because you're dressed in a wet suit."

"Rowan hid my catsuit."

Ah. Now, we're getting somewhere. Ashlyn only brings out the catsuit when she's ready to pull an epic prank. I should probably be relieved she's knocking on my door. She never knocks on the door of the unsuspecting victims of her pranks.

"Your husband hid your catsuit?"

"Or it got shrunk in the washing machine." She shrugs. "Either way."

"I'm glad I asked."

She pretends not to understand my sarcasm. "I know, right? Who would think you have to handwash a catsuit? But now you know."

"What prank are you pulling tonight?"

"I think you mean what prank are *we* pulling tonight."

"I'm not pulling a prank tonight." I lift my hand to show her the cut I got today.

She snorts. "As if a little scratch is going to stop you. Remember the time you did the high school prank with a concussion?"

It's hard to forget the police arresting you while you're throwing your guts up in the bushes in front of the high school. At least, the cop held back my hair. After he cuffed me.

"Who are we pranking?" There's no sense in bothering to fight Ashlyn. She always gets her way.

"Who do you think?" She waggles her eyebrows.

"I didn't think you were serious about pulling a prank on Riley."

And maybe Riley isn't such a bad guy after all. Did he fool me into thinking he loves me? Yes. But he took care of my injury today. If I didn't know he's a total ass, I would have swooned at how sweet he was when he blew on my cut. But I know the truth and no swooning was involved.

Ashlyn throws back her head and barks out a laugh. She laughs and laughs as she slaps her thighs. "You are hilarious! What's rule number one of this friendship?"

"Ashlyn's always right."

"Rule number two?"

"Don't forget rule number one."

"Rule number three?"

"Never get caught."

She throws her hands in the air. "Fine. I'll tell you." Note – patience is not a virtue in Ashlyn's book. "We never back down when a man hurts us."

This right here is why I didn't tell Ashlyn about Riley. Besides the whole embarrassed about a man ghosting me thing. And maybe feeling like a fool for falling in love with someone over the course of seven short days.

I cross my arms over my chest. "Say I agree to this."

"Yeah!"

"I didn't agree yet."

"But you will."

She's right, so I don't bother correcting her. "No illegal activities."

"Define illegal."

"Any activity that could end up with me spending the night in jail."

She huffs. "You always act like being in jail is a bad thing."

"To most people, it is."

"Most people are also boring."

I could stand here all night arguing with Ashlyn. But I know the truth. There's no way I'm getting out of this. I sigh.

"I'll get the glitter."

She holds up a bag. "Already covered."

"I thought you were out of glitter," I say as we walk toward Riley's house.

And, no, I'm not stalking him. I know where he lives because this is a small town and I know where everyone lives. I don't bike by his house ten times a day and wish he wasn't an asshole. Not this girl.

"I managed to find some I forgot about."

I don't believe her. Ashlyn doesn't forget about glitter but there's no use questioning her. She tells you what she tells you. Questioning her is a waste of breath.

"This is a nice house," she says when we stop on the sidewalk in front of Riley's place. "Why is Mr. Should Know Better Than To Hurt My Friend working as a handyman when he can afford this?"

I shrug. "Maybe he likes working with his hands."

She bumps my hip. "Is he good with his hands?"

"He's a decent handyman as far as I can tell."

"I wasn't referring to his handyman work and you know it."

I do. I'm also not answering her real question. Unlike everyone else in this town, I understand the definition of privacy.

"Come on." She grabs my hand and tugs me toward the house. "It looks like a basement window is open."

I drag my feet. "I thought we agreed to no illegal activities. Breaking into a basement is illegal."

"Nope. If the window is open, you're not breaking."

"But—"

She cuts me off. "When did you become such a fuddy duddy?"

"Maybe I grew up."

"Ha! And you didn't laugh yourself silly when I accidentally farted the other day."

"Accidentally? When a fart lasts for more than five seconds, it's not an accident."

"Still. Grown-ups don't laugh about farts."

"Grown-ups also don't use the word grown-ups. They say adults."

She shrugs – which is Ashlyn code for I know I lost this argument but I'm not admitting it – and lifts the basement window. "After you."

I give up fighting and shimmy through the window.

"Hey, Peace," Ashlyn calls.

Damn. I should have remembered the cop is Riley's half-brother and checked to make sure he wasn't visiting before I crawled into the basement. Whatever happens, I'm blaming Ashlyn.

"What are you doing?" Peace asks.

"Out for an evening stroll. It's a lovely night for a stroll."

"In a wetsuit?"

I knew the wetsuit was a bad idea.

"It's cold outside. I thought it'd keep me warm."

"Is it working?"

"Is what working?"

"Is the wetsuit keeping you warm, Ashlyn?"

"Um."

"Do I need to call Rowan?"

"No!" she screeches. "Ahem. I mean no. Why would you call Rowan?"

"Because you're obviously up to no good."

"Rowan isn't my keeper!"

"Hold on. I've got him on speed dial."

Ashlyn's face appears in the window. "Here." She throws the bag at me. I miss it and it lands on the floor with a thunk next to me. "You're on your own." She slams the window shut.

Hell's bells. How am I going to get out of here? I can't reach the basement window on my own. I was counting on my friend to give me a boost.

Don't panic, Moon. I can creep up the stairs and out of the house without Riley figuring out I was ever here. He won't notice since he sleeps like a drunken sailor out on shore leave. Unless he's not sleeping yet. I check my watch. Crap. It's barely nine o'clock.

It appears I'm stuck in this dark basement for at least another hour. The ambient light flowing through the window casts a shadow over the room. I shiver.

I amend my earlier statement. I'm stuck in this *creepy* basement while I wait for my ex-boyfriend – who I still love because I'm an idiot whose heart doesn't know how to unleash itself from a man – to fall asleep. My life has turned into the set-up for some cheesy romance movie.

I pick up the bag. Whoa. This weighs way more than glitter should. I open it and nearly gag from the smell of rotting fish. Freaking Ashlyn. I never should have trusted her when she said she had extra glitter laying around.

That does it. I'm not staying down here another second. I find the stairs and begin to creep up them. The second tread creaks and I freeze. I count to sixty but when no one rushes into the basement to confront me, I continue.

By the time I reach the top of the stairs, I can feel sweat gathering between my breasts despite how cold it is in the basement. I grasp the handle and twist before slowly pulling the door toward me.

"I was wondering how long you would wait before you came upstairs," Riley says. I scream and throw the bag at him.

"Ah!" I shout as I dash past him toward freedom.

An arm bands around my waist and stops me before I can reach the front door. "It's all Ashlyn's fault. I didn't do anything wrong. Don't call the cops. My back can't survive those horrible beds and I'm allergic to orange."

Riley picks me up and carries me to the living room where he deposits me on the sofa. He stands over me with his hands on his hips.

"You want to tell me why you're breaking into my house?" he demands in a gruff voice despite how the corners of his lips are tipped up in an almost there smile.

"Technically, it was the basement and there was a window open."

He digs his phone out of his pocket. "Try again."

"Pranking is a time honored Winter Falls tradition."

"Then, you won't mind if I call Peace to confirm."

"No!" I lunge for the phone.

Chapter 7

RILEY

I hold my phone in the air and Moon jumps up and down to try and grab it. I try to ignore how her breasts bounce as she jumps.

I fail. It's impossible not to notice her perky breasts when they're right there begging me to touch and massage them. To put my mouth on them. To suck her nipples. My cock hardens at the memory of how she goes wild when I play with her breasts.

"I won't call the police," I say before Moon can notice how much I want her. I don't think she'll appreciate me being hard when she's worried about spending the night in jail.

"Good. I guess I'll go home now."

I point to the sofa and growl, "Sit down."

She plops onto the sofa and crosses her arms over her chest causing her breasts to push up. She's not helping alleviate the hardness in my pants.

"What are you doing here?"

"It was an accident."

"You crawled through my basement window on accident?"

"It's all Ashlyn's fault."

I cough to hide my amusement with this situation.

"What were you hoping to accomplish in my basement?"

"It was supposed to be a glitter prank but Ashlyn didn't bring glitter. She brought a rotting fish."

"Rotting fish?" I stride toward the hallway where the bag Moon threw at me is on the floor. I pick it up but I don't need to open it to know what's in there. The stench gives it away.

I throw the bag in the garbage on my back porch before returning to the living room to find Moon trying to sneak out. I sigh.

"I thought we agreed you wouldn't sneak out."

She snorts. "I would never agree to not sneak out."

"What were you planning to do with glitter?"

"I can't tell you. It's proprietary information."

"Are you always this big of a troublemaker?"

"Are you always this much of a hard ass?"

I smirk. "As I recall, you love my hard ass." To be precise, she loves to dig her nails into it while I sink into her.

She rolls her eyes, but the blush staining her cheeks tells me she remembers how much she enjoys my ass. "Whatever."

I decide not to push her. I'm learning Moon doesn't react well to being pushed. "If you can't tell me what you were doing with the glitter, can you tell me why you were planning to prank me?"

"Girl code."

Another dead end.

"I didn't know you had a dog."

I frown at the strange turn of the conversation. "I don't."

She motions to the corner where the dog is lying in his dog bed.

Oh, him. "He showed up one day and won't go away."

She raises her eyebrows. "So, you bought him a doggy bed and a blanket and a chew toy?"

I shrug. "He was lonely."

"And now he's your dog."

"He's not my dog."

The dog lets out a loud fart in his sleep.

Moon's nose scrunches and she waves a hand in front of her face. "What in the world are you feeding him?"

"I bought the dog food the guy in the store recommended."

She shakes her head and tsks. "You didn't ask Juniper for advice?"

"Juniper?"

I don't recall meeting anyone named Juniper, but I've met a whole lot of people in Winter Falls and I can't possibly remember them all. I seriously think I know more people in this small town after living here for a month than I do in the city of San Diego where I lived for thirty years.

"She manages the wildlife refuge outside of town. Total animal nut. She's also engaged to Maverick Langston."

She's kidding. "The Maverick Langston?"

She rolls her eyes. "You might want to wipe the drool from your mouth."

I snap my mouth shut. "A movie star lives in Winter Falls?"

"Yep. And a former NFL quarterback."

"I can't believe Elder and Miller never told me any of this."

She taps her chin. "Hmm… Could it be because you were on the outs with them over them moving to a small town? Because you'd never – and this is a direct quote – 'consider moving to a small town'."

Damnit. I don't want to discuss this any more than I want to tell her why I ghosted her. Can't she be happy with me admitting I made a mistake? Most women love it when a man admits he made a mistake. Naturally, I had to pick the one woman who isn't satisfied with a simple admission of guilt.

"I had my reasons for not wanting to move away from San Diego."

She sighs and stands. "I'm sure you did. Have a good night."

Dread rushes through me at the idea of her leaving. I finally have her in my house. I don't want her to ever leave. "You're leaving?"

"What do you want me to do? Play with farty dog? Hate to break it to you, but lazy bones isn't moving anytime soon."

I glance over at the dog. He's laying on his back with his pudgy legs sticking straight up into the air. He's done for the night. I'll have to fight him to get him to go outside for his last potty break. But it's happening. I'm not cleaning dog piss off of my floors again.

"We could watch a movie."

She pauses and I cough to hide my smile. Moon loves movies. "What movie?"

"*Anchorman.*"

She narrows her eyes on me. "You have my all-time favorite movie?"

"And *Anchorman 2.*"

"The sequel is never as good as the first movie."

I shrug. "No problem. We'll stick to watching *Anchorman* and skip the sequel."

"Why would I watch a movie with you? We're not exactly friends."

We're way more than friends, but I keep those thoughts to myself. I prefer for my balls to remain attached to my body.

"I have that microwave butter popcorn you like."

She rushes to me and slaps her hands over my mouth. "Shush. Watch what you say." Her eyes dart around the room as if she's searching for intruders. "Microwaves are frowned upon in Winter Falls."

My brow furrows. "Why?" I mumble from behind her hands.

"Electricity consumption is too high."

I should have realized. Winter Falls goes a bit extreme when it comes to being green. I roll my eyes and she drops her hands to slap my chest. I want to capture her wrists but I stuff my hands in my pockets instead.

"Don't you dare say Winter Falls is weird. Having all kinds of rules to help protect the environment doesn't make us weird."

"Is it weird how the owner of the pet store likes to stroll around town naked?"

I met the famous Forest walking home from work today. Imagine my surprise when I happened upon a man walking his pets with no pants on in December. And those pets? They were squirrels.

"Don't exaggerate. Forest always wears shoes and a coat."

I could care less what the man wears. Was I surprised? Yes. Is it my business? No.

I drop the subject and dial up the temptation to Moon. "I also have some of the root beer you like."

"Pop and microwave popcorn. You're just dying to get a violation, aren't you?"

"Depends. Are you the one who's going to punish me?" I waggle my eyebrows.

"You won't be flirting when you have to spend the night in jail. Those beds are brutal."

"Stop exaggerating. You spent a total of two hours in jail."

Her nose wrinkles. "How do you… Never mind."

"I remember everything you told me, Moonbeam. Every single thing." So much for not pushing her anymore tonight.

"Whatever. Are we eating popcorn and watching a movie or what?"

I smirk. "I'll start the popcorn."

She wags a finger at me. "And don't think you've won. This isn't me forgiving you and giving you a second chance. This isn't even us becoming friends. This is me taking advantage of the one person in town who has a microwave and isn't afraid to use it."

"And root beer. Don't forget the root beer."

By the time I return to the living room with the popcorn and root beer, she has the movie cued up and the dog is on the sofa with its chin propped on her lap.

"How did the dog get on the sofa?"

The dog is the laziest creature I've ever encountered. Although, my experience is limited as I've never had a pet before.

"I carried him." She squishes his face with her hands. "Isn't he adorable? What's his name?"

I set the popcorn and drinks on the coffee table before joining her on the sofa. "He doesn't have a name. He's dog."

She gasps. "Riley Bragg! Don't tell me you adopted a pet and you didn't give him a name?"

"I didn't adopt a pet. He's not my dog."

"We've been through this. He's your dog."

"Whatever."

She scratches the dog behind his ears and he moans. "What shall we name you? Farty Dog? Nah. Too long. Lazy bones? What about Charlie?" He licks her hand. "Charlie it is!"

"Did you just name my dog?"

"Ha! I knew he was your dog. Charlie and Riley sitting on the sofa. F-A-R-T-I-N-G."

"I am not farting!" I exclaim but I don't care what she says about me. She's here. In my home. With me. Laughing and joking. This is what I want. This is what I intend to have.

Watch out, Moon Star. I'm not giving up into I get what I want.

Chapter 8

"COME ON. STOP LOLLYGAGGING." Ashlyn threads her arm through mine and pulls me toward the entrance of the courthouse.

"I'm not lollygagging. I'm tired and muscles I didn't know existed hurt. Hell, my eyeballs hurt." I sigh. "I want to soak in a bath for a month."

"Ahem. You know baths are bad for the environment," Ashlyn's sister, Lilac, says as she joins us.

Lilac is an environmental engineer. She spearheads most of the town's environmental initiatives. Currently, she's working on a biomass power plant outside of town.

"Which is why I'm not in one right now." I lie.

I'm not in my bathtub because attendance at the Winter Falls monthly business meeting is basically mandatory. If I didn't attend, the entire gossip gal gang would show up at my house after the meeting with chicken soup to heal whatever's ailing me because the only reason you skip a meeting is an illness. Sore as hell muscles don't count.

We walk into the courthouse and down the hall toward the meeting room. In front of the entrance, the current mayor, Eden, is staring down Riley's brother, Miller.

Riley. Damnit. Is he here?

I haven't prepared myself to see him tonight. I need to fortify my shields against the charming man who adopted a farty, lazy dog. The man who apparently remembers every single thing I told him during our short week together, including my favorite movie and snack food.

Eden smirks at Miller. "Too bad we couldn't get the expansion of the building for *Naked Falls Brewing* approved before my term as mayor finished."

Miller growls at her. "I know you did everything in your power to stop the expansion."

Her eyes widen and she places a hand on her chest. "Me? I would never."

He gets all up in her face. "I have your number, Ms. Innocent."

Ashlyn nudges me. "Have you placed your bet yet?"

"Bet? What are you going on about now?"

She motions toward Miller and Eden. "For when the enemies become lovers."

"Tsk. Tsk. You know better, Ashlyn. We limit our matchmaking projects to one at a time," Sage announces from behind us.

I know she's referring to Project Do Over, which is what the gossip gals have named their attempt to match Riley and me back together. I could argue with her. Tell her Riley and I will never be back together.

But I'm not going to waste my breath. If Sage doesn't want to listen to what you have to say, she pretends not to hear you.

"We had to recalculate the odds after last night. Movie and popcorn. How romantic." Feather sighs.

I glare at her. "Were you spying on me?"

"Why? Did you do anything worth spying on?"

I throw my hands in the air. "I need a beer," I announce and stomp away.

"Get a bucket!" Ashlyn shouts after me.

I flick my hand in acknowledgement. It might seem odd to have drinks and snacks at a business meeting, but this is Winter Falls. We excel at odd.

"Hey Moonbeam," Riley greets as he joins the line for popcorn and beer behind me.

"Hi," I grunt while keeping my gaze aimed at the back of the person in front of me. Maybe if I don't look at him, I won't be susceptible to his charm. It's worth a try.

"I didn't expect to see you here tonight."

I groan. "Are you going to use all the lame chat up lines on me until I talk to you? Because I have to tell you, it won't work."

"You're talking to me now, aren't you?"

Crap. I am. I also turned around to look at him. I suck at ignoring him.

He brushes a finger over my cheek and goosebumps erupt on my skin. *Damn it, body. He barely touched me. Control yourself!*

"You look tired."

I rear back. "Tired? Are you saying I look like shit?"

"You're gorgeous. You could never look like shit," he says and several women in line sigh.

A fist wraps around my stomach and anger bursts through me. Damnit. I recognize this feeling. It's jealousy. I don't want anyone sighing at my man. *Whoa, Moon. He's not your man. He left you, remember?*

"Go sit down. I'll get you your beer and popcorn."

"How do you know I want beer and popcorn?"

He cocks an eyebrow. I huff. Of course, he knows. He apparently remembers everything.

"I want a bucket of beer," I order and march away before I can pounce on him to show all the other ladies in line he's mine. He's not mine. Not anymore.

I find a seat in the front row with Ashlyn and her sisters. She has four of them. Plus, she adopted her four sisters-in-law as sisters. Meanwhile, I don't have one single sibling. I force those thoughts out of my mind. I don't feel sorry for myself. I don't.

"Where's our beer and popcorn?" Ashlyn glares at my empty hands.

"It's being delivered."

She stands and scans the room. The second she spots Riley a smile spreads over her face. "Awesome. My evil plans are working."

I poke her. "You're supposed to be on my side."

"I am! I want you to get lots and lots of orgasms."

Her husband groans. "Dream girl."

"What? Do you need reassuring? Dude, you give the best most awesome orgasms in the world."

Rowan shakes his head before walking off with their baby strapped to his chest. I have no interest in the man. He's my best friend's husband. But I can't deny how sexy the six-foot-five-inch former NFL quarterback appears when he's cuddling his baby girl.

"Hey!" Ashlyn shouts after her husband. "We're supposed to share Patience."

Patience is their daughter. Considering Ashlyn has zero patience, her naming her daughter Patience is a mystery.

Riley arrives with a bucket of beer and a bag of popcorn.

Juniper jumps to her feet. "Here. You can have my spot," she says with a wink to me.

"You don't have to go," I call after her.

She jiggles her phone at me. "Maverick called. He's on his way home." She wiggles her eyebrows. "I need to prepare."

"Don't act like you're going to put on some sexy lingerie when I know you're off to clean up the house. I lived with you. I know how messy you are," Ashlyn yells after her sister.

"Is she married to Maverick Langston?" Riley asks as he sits down.

"Nope. They're engaged. She's having a hard time planning the wedding," I say.

"Which is code for she's afraid he'll change his mind about marrying her," Ashlyn explains.

Riley meets my gaze. "If he proposed, he wants to marry her."

"Oh boy. Is it hot in here? I'm feeling warm." Ashlyn fans herself.

I break my connection with Riley to glare at Ashlyn.

She widens her eyes in innocence. What a joke! She hasn't been innocent a day in her life. "What? I can't help it if the heat between the two of you gave me a hot flash."

Eden stomps past us on her way to the front of the room. "Let's get this shit show started."

Everyone settles in their seats, and Ashlyn passes out the beer. "The word of the day is no."

"What does she mean? Word of the day?" Riley asks as he twists off the top of a beer and hands it to me.

"Anytime someone says the word of the day, we have to drink."

"Anytime someone says 'no', we have to drink?" he asks.

"Drink!" Ashlyn shouts and I take a sip of my beer.

"Winter Falls is fun," Riley says.

Is he serious? He didn't want to live in a small town before. He was adamant, although I don't know why since he refused to explain his apparent hatred of small towns. But there's no sign of hatred now.

Bang! Bang! Bang!

"I now call the final meeting of the Winter Falls business community of the year to order." Eden nods to Lilac. "Since this is my last meeting as the mayor, our first order of business is to choose a new mayor."

"Whoo! Hoo!" Miller shouts from the back of the room.

Riley leans close to whisper, "Why is my brother excited?"

I close my eyes and will myself to ignore how his breath on my skin feels. How I can smell his wood and oil scent. I clear my throat. "Because Eden and Miller hate each other."

He frowns. "I admit my brother's a grump, but he doesn't hate people."

"Trust me. They hate each other."

"It's only a matter of time before they bump uglies," Ashlyn adds. Except she doesn't whisper. She yells.

Eden glares at her. "Behave."

"Why start now?" Ashlyn asks before throwing a wad of popcorn in her mouth.

Riley chuckles. "I understand why the two of you are best friends."

I elbow him. "Behave.

He wiggles his eyebrows. "Why start now?"

"Can I have your attention, please?" Lilac scans the room, and everyone immediately quiets down. No one wants to get on the wrong side of her since she's the town comptroller and thus controls the town's purse strings.

"We will now pick next year's mayor. The same rules apply as always. If your name is picked, you cannot turn the position down unless you were the mayor in the previous year. It is, however, allowed to procure a substitute. The substitute will not be compensated in any way."

She narrows her eyes on her sister, Ellery.

"Why are you looking at me? I didn't compensate Ashlyn when she substituted for me."

"You didn't pay for her to get a massage?"

"She's my sister. I'm allowed to buy gifts for her."

"Especially since I'm such an awesome sister and was the best mayor this town has ever seen," Ashlyn adds.

"No you weren't," Lilac argues and Ashlyn shouts, "Drink!"

"Would anyone like to double check all of the business owners' names are in the hat?" Lilac asks.

"Did she say hat?" Riley asks.

"Yep. We believe in equality in Winter Falls. There's no election for mayor," I explain.

Lilac holds the hat out to Eden. "If you would do the honors."

"With pleasure." She smiles as her hand plunges into the hat. She removes a piece of paper and hands it to Lilac.

"And the new mayor of Winter Falls is," Lilac glances in my direction, "Moon Star."

I groan. Great. As if I'm not busy enough as it is.

Riley stands and pulls me to his feet. "Congratulations!"

He wraps his arms around me and draws me flush to his hard body. I circle his waist with my arms. Not because I want to but because otherwise my hands would be trapped between our bodies and it would be awkward.

As soon as my arms envelop him, he sighs. "I missed you, Moonbeam," he whispers before kissing my hair.

Crap. Crap. Crap. What am I doing? I shouldn't be hugging the man who can't be trusted to not abandon me. And I definitely shouldn't be enjoying it and thinking it feels like home. Nope. This is not home.

Chapter 9

"I DON'T KNOW WHY we had to leave my house. I had beer and wine and snacks," I whine as Ashlyn drags me toward the entrance of *Electric Vibes.*

"It's pub quiz night. You can't let our team down."

"We don't have a team." I'm not lying. We don't.

Ashlyn's on the 'dream team' – her words, not mine – with the rest of her sisters and their partners. Once upon a time, the West sisters were hell raisers. Now, they're all settled down and three of them have children.

Although, Ashlyn being a married mother hasn't settled her down any. No matter how much her husband tries to tame her, she'll always be a wild child.

"We do tonight!"

"Who's on the team? I vote for Lilac."

Ashlyn's sister is super smart. She knows everything about everything. Except sports. But Ashlyn's a whizz at sports questions – the result of spending years being obsessed with football in order to catch a glimpse of her crush, Rowan. He actually thought he had a chance to keep her at arm's length. Silly man.

"Lilac's not here. It's single's night."

I freeze on the sidewalk. "Single's night?"

Electric Vibes has never had a single's night before. Single's night isn't exactly necessary in a small town where everyone knows everyone.

"Cassandra came up with the idea," Ashlyn claims as she tugs on my arm.

I keep my feet planted and narrow my eyes on her. "Cassandra came up with the idea?"

As if I can't smell an Ashlyn idea a mile away. They have a certain stench to them. Usually, it's danger. Today it's just plain pushy.

"Cassandra is the owner of the pub. I don't tell her what to do."

Cassandra is Ashlyn's sister-in-law. Cassandra's boyfriend, Cedar, and Ashlyn's husband, Rowan, are brothers. It sounds confusing, but everyone's intertwined in some way in a small town. Except me. I'm all by myself over here. No parents. No siblings. No entanglements.

Where did those thoughts come from? I usually don't feel sorry for myself, but lately, I've been feeling awful lonely and sad about being lonely. This is not me. I'm Ashlyn's trusty sidekick. Always up for a fun time and a good pranking.

I allow Ashlyn to pull me into the bar and notice the place is decorated for Christmas. Ah, now I remember why I've been feeling lonely lately. The dreaded holiday alone season is upon yes. Yippee. Sarcasm intended.

"There's our team." Ashlyn points to a table where our friends – Eden, Harmony, and Soleil – are sitting. All of whom are single.

"You weren't kidding about this being single's night."

"Nope." She shoves me toward the table. "I'll order a pitcher of margaritas."

"Who dragged you here?" I ask Harmony as I settle in the seat next to her. Harmony doesn't care much for social gatherings or big events.

"Juniper said she'd clean out Lucy's enclosure."

Lucy is a llama at the wildlife refuge where Harmony works as Juniper's assistant.

"What else?" No way Harmony, the insane animal lover, would be forced to a single's night at the bar to get out of cleaning a llama's enclosure.

She leans close to whisper, "Juniper promised me an advance DVD of Maverick's new romantic comedy."

"What?" Ashlyn screeches. "My sister promised you a Maverick DVD before me?"

Uh oh. The people of Winter Falls will insist on a private screening if they find out Juniper has access to a DVD of Maverick's latest film.

The previous time this happened did not go well. The gossip gals posted rave reviews on all the movie review websites after watching the movie. Which sounds sweet, but Maverick didn't have permission to share the DVD. The studio execs were pissed with a capital P at him.

Time for a distraction.

"What is that?" I shout my question while motioning toward the pitcher of bright red liquid Ashlyn's carrying. "I thought you were getting margaritas."

"It's Ponche de Granada," Cassandra yells from behind the bar. "You're welcome."

"I could use a drink," Eden mumbles before pouring herself a glass.

"Ah, what's wrong, Eden? Haven't gotten your corn ground by Miller yet?" Ashlyn asks with a bat of her eyelashes.

Eden glares at her. "Miller can jump off Winter Falls for all I care."

Winter Falls isn't merely the name of the town. It's the name of the waterfall on the river near town. The water is freezing cold, which is how it got the name, Winter Falls.

Eden sips on her drink but ends up sputtering and coughing. "Warning. Cassandra is trying to get us drunk."

"There is no try," Cassandra shouts from across the room.

Ashlyn elbows me. "Don't look now," she whisper–shouts, "but you have an admirer."

I follow her gaze to where she's pointing across the room. Riley is sitting at a booth with his brothers, but he isn't paying a bit of attention to his family. He's too busy staring at me. When his gaze catches mine, he smiles and winks. I roll my eyes and glance away.

Ashlyn pokes me. "I told you not to look."

"You also pointed."

Lennon taps on the microphone. "Shall we get started?"

Lennon is the former owner of *Electric Vibes,* but he still helps Cassie out behind the bar and is usually the MC when there's a pub quiz.

"Usual rules apply," he says. "The first person to raise their hand will be called on for the answer. If the answer is correct, we'll—"

Ashlyn cuts him off. "We know the rules."

He glares at her. "Then, you know you can't participate. Tonight is for singles only."

"I'm here as moral support."

He snorts. "If you're here for moral support, my favorite band is The Beach Boys."

Forest gasps. "Take it back, Lennon! Take it back!"

I roll my eyes. We're, I don't know how many decades, removed from the hippie generation, and yet the rivalry between The Beatles and The Beach Boys will never die in Winter Falls.

Ashlyn motions for us to lean in close. "I don't need to participate. We've got the best team here. Eden will answer all plant related questions. Moon has the food and cooking category. Harmony has animals. And Soleil has everything else."

"If I see you open your mouth one more time, Ashlyn West—"

Ashlyn cuts Lennon off. "It's Ashlyn Hansley now."

He ignores her interruption to finish. "I will disqualify your team."

"There's no need to threaten the team just because you know this is the best team in the house."

"Are we ready to begin?" he asks. When everyone nods, he reads the first question. "Approximately how many nerve endings does the clitoris have?"

Everyone in the room looks to Soleil to answer the question.

Her cheeks darken. "Knitting vibrator covers doesn't make me a sex expert."

I snort. She totally knows the answer. "What's the answer?"

"Approximately 8,000. The penis has a mere 4,000."

"Women rock!" Ashlyn lifts her hands in victory. Naturally, she forgets she's holding a glass filled with Ponche de Granada and it spills all over my top.

"Whoo hoo! Wet t-shirt contest." She claps and starts humming *Blurred Lines.*

I stand. "If you did this on purpose, I will kill you. And not in your sleep. I will tie you to a chair and make you listen to a woman drag her nails down a chalkboard until your ears are bleeding."

She does a full-body shiver. "You're cruel, moon pie."

"And you're a troublemaker, Ashlyn Bashlyn."

She smiles. "Thank you."

"Whatever," I mumble as I stomp toward the bathroom.

Out of the corner of my eye, I notice Riley stand. Great. I always enjoy being embarrassed in front of the man I love but can't have. It really makes my holiday season.

I hurry into the bathroom, but as soon as I see my reflection in the mirror I slow down. There's no way I'm getting pomegranate juice out of this sweater. Red juice and green sweater equals disaster. Unless I'm trying to resemble a drunk elf. In which case, nailed it!

I dry myself as best I can before leaving the restroom and walk smack dab into Riley.

"Are you stalking me?"

"How am I stalking you?"

"You followed me to the restrooms."

He cocks an eyebrow. "I did? Maybe I was on my way to the men's room when you slammed into me."

"Yeah, right. And you didn't come to the bar tonight to see me."

"And miss out on another crazy Winter Falls event?"

Crazy? I narrow my eyes on him. "If you don't like Winter Falls, you should go live somewhere else." Sure, he'll take my heart with him, but I can survive without a heart. Probably.

"I happen to like Winter Falls. One of the residents in particular." He winks.

"Oh, my god. Will you stop already? We are never ever getting back together."

He crowds me until my back is pressed against the wall.

"Moonbeam, we are definitely getting back together. I will earn a second chance with you."

"How?" Crap. I didn't mean to ask that.

"By showing up. Every. Single. Day."

Damnit. It's a good answer. But I don't believe him.

"I don't believe you."

He tucks a strand of hair behind my ear before trailing a finger from my ear down my neck. The feel of his calloused fingers has me nearly melting into the floor. I know how those fingers feel touching other parts of my body. The best parts. The most sensitive parts. I shiver.

"I'll prove it to you."

What? Prove what? I glance up to discover his attention is focused on my lips. Suddenly, my lips feel awful dry. I lick the bottom one and he moans.

His head descends but before his lips can meet mine someone claps at the end of the hallway.

"My evil plan is working."

Ashlyn's announcement reminds me of where I am. In the very public hallway of the only bar in town. Was I about to kiss Riley? Crap.

"I'm leaving," I announce before hurrying toward the back door and going outside where I gulp big breaths of air into my lungs.

He's not to be trusted. His charm is all a lie.

Don't fall for it, Moon. You know better. Riley's already abandoned you once. Once is enough.

Chapter 10

Dim your brights! You're not a Christmas tree ~ Text from Elder to Riley

RILEY

"Is this weird?" I ask as I walk up the sidewalk toward the home of Eagle and Clementine.

We've been here before to meet our half-brother's parents, but celebrating Christmas with the woman your dad impregnated feels odd. Kind of as if we're cheating on our mother.

Miller grunts in agreement while Elder and Brody shrug. The door flies open. Too late now anyway.

"You're here!" Clementine smiles at us. "Come in. Come in."

"Merry Christmas, my Clementine darling," I greet and kiss her cheek. She giggles.

"Are you flirting with my mom?" Peace asks from where he's standing inside the hallway.

I shrug. "I can't help it if your mother is a—"

"Say it and I will slap handcuffs on you so fast it'll make your head spin," he grumbles.

"Calm down, Johnny Law," Olivia says from beside him. "Flirting with your mom isn't illegal. Although," she winks at me, "he is pretty handy with the handcuffs."

Elder slaps his hands over his ears. "I don't want to hear about my sister having sex. Gross."

Brody barks out a laugh. "No wonder he's alone. He thinks sex is gross."

"Who says I'm alone?" Elder waggles his eyebrows.

Brody raises his hand. "I do. I live with you. You haven't brought a woman home since I moved in."

Elder elbows him. "You don't live with me. You're crashing on my sofa."

"I fail to understand the difference."

"Where's Damon?" Clementine asks as she counts brothers.

"With Mom," Miller says. My brother hardly speaks, but now – when his words are going to hurt Clementine – he's feeling chatty?

"Oh my." Clementine clutches her chest. "Did he not feel welcome here? Do I need to phone him and apologize for offending him? I bought him a Christmas gift. Should I mail it? Is he returning to Winter Falls?"

Olivia smiles at Peace. "I didn't realize your mother is a drama queen."

He frowns. "She's usually not. It's the holidays."

"Bummer. I love a drama queen."

He throws an arm around her. "You would, troublemaker."

"Drama and trouble aren't the same thing."

"Don't worry, my Clementine darling. Damon is boring any-way. You've got the best of the Bragg brothers here today." I wink.

Peace steps toward me. "I told you to stop flirting with my mom."

"It's not my fault your mother is gorgeous. I can't help myself."

"I can help you."

He lunges toward me, but Brody catches him before he can reach me.

"The only person allowed to beat up my twin on Christmas day is me."

Olivia claps and bounces on her toes. "This is the best Christmas ever. Sexy brothers beating each other up is way better than sisters being catty to each other. Can you remove your shirts before you continue?"

Peace growls at her. "You're not supposed to be staring at men who aren't me."

"It's not my fault your brothers are handsome," she says and I high-five her.

"This is supposed to be the best Christmas because it's our first Christmas together," Peace claims.

"Ah. You two are adorable," I say and wink at Olivia. Peace grunts before launching at me again.

Elder chuckles as he holds Peace back. "You obviously didn't grow up with brothers."

Clementine sniffs. "I wanted to give him siblings, but ..."

Eagle enters the hallway. He studies the situation before hauling his wife into his arms. "Emmy, please don't cry on Christmas. And, Peace, stop fighting with your brothers."

"They started it," Peace mumbles.

Elder rubs his knuckles over Peace's head. "You're a quick learner."

Peace shoves Elder away, but before they can get in a scuffle, Eagle steps between them. "I have the appetizers laid out in the living room."

"You don't need to tell me twice," Brody says and rushes off. Miller grunts and follows him.

"Hey!" Elder shouts. "Don't eat everything before I get there."

The living room resembles the set for one of those Hallmark Christmas movies you can't avoid if you switch on your television anytime in the month of December. There's a Christmas tree with a load of presents underneath it, stockings are hung on the mantle, wreaths of all shapes and sizes decorate the walls, and Christmas cookies are laid out on every flat surface.

Miller reaches for a cookie and Clementine slaps it out of his hand. "Those are for after dinner."

"Yes, ma'am."

"Suck up," Elder utters under his breath.

"Is that a pigs in a blanket wreath?" I point to the wreath that is seriously made out of a bunch of pigs in a blanket. "I think I love you, Clementine."

Peace glares at me. "Dad is the cook in the family. Not Mom."

"I can still love your mom, can't I?"

Clementine pats my arm. "You are a charmer, aren't you?"

Elder barks out a laugh. "Except his charm is getting him nowhere with the woman he wants."

I ignore him and bite into a pig in a blanket. They can talk shit all they want. While they're gabbing like old women, I'll finish the appetizers.

"And it's making him grumpy," Brody adds.

Miller grunts in agreement.

"Could it be he's mooning over someone?" Elder asks.

Olivia bursts into laughter. "He's mooning over Moon. Awesome! These guys are such fun."

Peace wraps an arm around her. "I'm fun."

She pats his stomach. "Sure, you are, Johnny Law. Sure, you are."

I'm reaching for a piece of cheesy bread from the bread bites formed into a Christmas tree – Eagle and Clementine seriously went all out with this spread – when I hear a rattle. I glance around the room but I can't locate the sound.

I bite into the bread and moan. It's cheesy and herby and utterly delicious. But I pause in my chewing when I hear the rattle again. I swallow the bread before starting to roam around the room to figure out where the sound is coming from.

The rattle occurs again when I'm next to the Christmas tree. I scan the gifts and notice one of them is moving.

"Brody, tell me you didn't."

He widens his eyes and feigns innocence. "Didn't what?"

Peace steps between us. "What's going on?"

"Brody's a prankster."

"And?" He motions for me to continue. "I need more information."

I indicate a present under the tree. "One of the presents is moving."

Peace kneels at the tree. "It's addressed to you, Riley."

Of course, it is. Why did I have to be born a twin? And why is my twin Brody? What did I do to deserve this?

"Mom, did you buy Riley a present?"

Clementine nods. "Of course. I bought all you boys presents."

Peace slides the suspect gift forward. "Is this Riley's gift?"

Her brow wrinkles. "No. My wrapping paper has snowmen on it. Not." She squints at the paper to read it. "A message stating Merry Christmas Asshole." She scowls.

Crap. It's as I suspected. Brody's up to his old tricks.

Brody skips to the tree. "It's time to pass out gifts. Yeah!" He lifts the box and hands it to me. "Merry Christmas, Ass—"

"I'd stop there if I were you," Peace grumbles.

I glare at Brody. "And if I end up in the emergency room, I will kill you."

"Geez. Let it go already. It was one time."

"It was more than one time and you know it."

"Correction. You only stayed overnight one time. The rest don't count."

He can't be serious. "Getting stitches doesn't count?"

"Nope."

"A concussion doesn't count?"

"Nope."

"Why do I bother with you?"

"Because I'm the awesome twin." He taps the box. "Open it. Open it."

The box rattles again. I lift the lid off and a cat flies out of the box straight onto my face. His nails dig into my cheeks and I drop the box before grabbing the cat. I try to tug him off of me, but he's not giving up his hold on my face without a fight.

I yank on his neck as hard as I can and he lets go right before I lose my grip on him. He flies through the air and lands on the Christmas tree.

"Shit." I scramble after the furry devil along with Peace. We both try to catch the furball, but he climbs higher up the tree and out of our grasp. He swats the angel to the ground and perches on top of the tree as if he's the tree-topper.

Every time I reach for him he swipes at me. I'm going to have scratches on my arms to match the ones on my face. I finally manage to catch him by the scruff of his neck. I hold him as far away from my body as I can as I pull him off the tree.

"What the hell am I supposed to do with him?"

"He'll make a great companion for your dog," Brody suggests.

"I don't have a dog."

"You bought that fart machine a doggy bed. He's yours now."

I'm not arguing about Charlie. "I meant what do I do to stop this crazy animal from destroying the entire Christmas tree."

"Too late," Olivia says and motions toward the ornaments smashed to bits on the ground.

"I got this." Peace throws a net over the cat and carries it out of the room.

"Did he just happen to have a net lying around?" Elder asks the room.

"It's a fishing net," Eagle answers.

"I'm sorry, Clementine. My brother is uncontrollable."

Tears gather in her eyes. Ah, crap. A crying mom is bad enough but on Christmas day? Hell is going to break loose. Eagle looks like he's ready to tear me and my brothers apart limb for limb.

"This is the best Christmas ever," Clementine exclaims.

"What?" Peace snarls as he returns to the living room. "My half-brothers are a bunch of nitwits who are completely inconsiderate of others."

Olivia laces her arm through Clementine's. "I'm with your mom. Best. Christmas. Ever."

They embrace before collapsing into giggles.

Brody puffs out his chest. "I'm the man."

I shove him. "You're an idiot."

"Boys!" Eagle shouts.

"Uh oh. He used his 'dad voice'," Elder mock whispers. "We're in trouble."

"I need to clean up my scratches," I say and march out of the room before I end up in a fight with my twin.

Chapter 11

Can I borrow your shovel? ~ Text from Moon to Ashlyn

I GROAN WHEN THERE'S a knock on the door. I'm all cuddled up on my sofa with my blanket watching a movie while I gorge myself on Christmas cookies and wine. The combination is one I invented myself and it's awesome. Follow me for more gourmet tips.

"I know you're home, Moon!" Riley shouts through the door.

"Awesome power of observation. Two points for you. Now, leave me alone."

"No way. It's Christmas."

"Wow! Your amazing powers of observation are blowing me over."

"Let me in."

"Why?"

Don't get me wrong. I'd love to let Riley in and continue where we left off at singles night. Heat flows to my core at the idea. But I can't. Because he can't be trusted to not desert me again. I'm not letting him fool me into falling in love with him again.

"I have your Christmas present."

Dang it. I've been dying to know what the present he tried to give me at Yule is.

"I know you're curious."

What is it with him and remembering everything about me? We spent one week together. Seven short days! I've had boyfriends who lasted for months but who couldn't remember the color of my eyes. They're brown by the way.

I throw my blanket off and stomp to the door.

"What the hell?" I ask when I notice how scratched up Riley is. "Did Charlie attack you?"

He snorts. "No. This was Brody's annual Christmas prank."

My brow wrinkles. "Brody scratched you?"

He lifts up the wrapped gift. "Can I come inside? I'll explain everything."

I was already itching to open the present and now I absolutely need to know why he's scratched up. He's using my curiosity against me. Dang it. I usually love a bit of deviousness – assuming I'm the one wielding it.

I wave him inside. He frowns as he scans the living room.

"Have a seat." I almost continue and offer him wine but I snap my mouth shut in time. He's not a welcomed guest here. He's here to give me a present and nothing else. We're not going to make out on my couch. A little scenario I may have daydreamed about a time or two.

"Where are your Christmas decorations?"

I shrug. "Probably in a box in the basement."

I haven't decorated for Christmas since I was seventeen and my parents said they'd visit for the holidays. I baked dozens of cookies, prepared a Christmas meal for a king, and waited. And waited. And waited. They never showed.

In fact, they've only been back to Winter Falls once since they left when I was sixteen. To attend my high school graduation. Yeah, I was shocked to look up and see them in the crowd, too.

The only other times I've seen my parents is when I've traveled to visit them. Which is usually a logistical nightmare as they don't like to stay in one place too long – it's too constricting – and don't feel it necessary to keep me informed about where they are even when they know I'm planning to visit!

"I want to pull you into my arms right now," Riley grumbles and I snap out of my reverie.

"Why?"

"Because you're hurting."

I shove those feelings of abandonment my parents left me with into the box I had specially made for them. "I'm not hurting."

"Don't lie to me."

I'm not going to discuss my feelings with him. "We're not friends."

"It felt awful friendly when you were in my arms the other day."

It didn't feel friendly to me. It felt like a whole lot more, which is why I need to shut down this conversation fast.

"You promised to explain where all the scratches came from." I study his face and wince. "Did you put antibiotic cream on them? Do you need a tetanus shot?"

He chuckles. "I don't think I need a tetanus shot from cat scratches."

"A cat did this to you? What did you do to her?"

"It was a him. I think. And I didn't do anything."

I cock my brow. In my experience, animals don't attack unless you attack them first. Except for the beaver that one time. But beavers are mean. How was I supposed to know that pile of sticks in the water was his home?

"I'm serious. Brody's the one who stuffed the cat into a box and left him in there for who knows how long. It wasn't me. But I'm the one who had to chase the little asshole before he destroyed the Christmas tree."

"Christmas tree? Box? I think you need to start at the beginning."

By the time Riley finishes telling me the story, I'm cracking up.

"And Clementine didn't kill you for destroying her perfect tree?"

He shrugs. "She thought it was hilarious. As did Olivia."

I snort. "Of course, Olivia did." I haven't known Olivia long – she only recently relocated to Winter Falls to be with the rest of her sisters – but what I do know of her, I like.

"You explained the scratches. Now, it's time for presents." I wiggle my fingers toward him. "Gimme. Gimme."

He hands me the wrapped package. "I hope you like it."

He sounds uncertain, which makes me love him more. No! I refuse to love him anymore. He's not to be trusted. He's been banished from The People Who Moon Loves List. Crossed right off it with a permanent marker.

I'm not one of those people who gently unwraps a gift so I can reuse the paper, although there is a rule about reusing gift paper in Winter Falls. Luckily, what no one knows can't lead to clean up duty after a festival.

I tear off the wrapping paper to reveal a sign that says *Moon's Diner.*

"Did you make this?" I ask as I caress the sign. The name appears to be burned into the wood and in the corner, there's a small waterfall representing Winter Falls. It's gorgeous.

"Yeah. I have a shop in my garage. I sell some items online."

"You never told me you're an artist."

His cheeks darken as he shrugs. "I'm not an artist. Woodworking isn't an art."

I hold up the sign. "Have you seen this? You're an artist."

"I'm glad you like it."

I hug the sign to my chest. "I love it. I hope I get to use it someday."

"Why wouldn't you be able to use it?"

I sigh. "Because the diner isn't open yet. I thought I would be open before Yule. Yule and Christmas are the best times of the year for a restaurant business. But am I open? No. I'm bleeding money."

Riley grasps my hands. "Will you let me help?"

"Dude, you're giving me a twenty percent discount. That's the definition of helping."

His thumbs stroke my inner wrists. I want to melt into the sofa and allow him to touch me all over. Which is why I should pull away from him. Kick him out of my house. And continue watching movies while gorging on Christmas cookies and wine all by myself.

But I don't want to be alone. I'm tired of being alone on Christmas day. I'm tired of being a family of one. I'm lonely. There! I said it.

"You want to watch a movie?" Add weak to the list of emotions I'm feeling.

He steals a sugar cookie from my tray and stuffs it in his mouth.

"I didn't say you can have a cookie."

His arm sweeps out to indicate the tray which contains at least two dozen cookies.

"You can't possibly eat all of these."

I totally can. "Whatever."

He grins and swipes a snowball. "What are we watching?"

I don't know what he's watching, but I can't tear my gaze away from him licking sugar off of his fingers. I want to be his fingers. I want him to lick me all over. I shiver as visions of him licking my bare skin during the week we were together flicker through my mind. Me spread out on the bed completely naked. Us laying on the beach after dark.

"Moonbeam, you okay? You look a little warm."

"My blanket is thermal."

He smirks. "You're not under your blanket now."

I look down. Damn. He's right. "I was before you came. I haven't cooled down yet."

"I can't help with cooling you down. Warming you up on the other hand? I excel in."

I throw a cookie at him and he catches it mid-air. "Yum. Gingerbread."

"If you want to watch a movie with me, you have to be quiet."

He chuckles. "Because you never talk during a movie."

I sniff and stick my nose in the air. "I don't."

I totally do. In my defense, I only talk during movies I've seen more than once. And the movie I'm currently watching – *Die Hard* – I might have seen a dozen times or more.

"Shush. The movie is starting."

I restart the movie and pour myself another glass of wine. Riley stands, strolls to the kitchen, and opens the refrigerator like he lives here. He pulls out a beer before sauntering back and joining me on the sofa.

I should yell at him for making himself at home. This isn't his home. We aren't friends. But when he sits in the middle of the sofa and I feel the heat of his body next to me, I can't remember why we're not friends. Why we're not more than friends.

Movie. Must watch movie.

"Moonbeam."

I swat at the noise.

"Ouch."

My eyes fly open to discover Riley smiling down at me.

"What are you doing?"

"I didn't want to go home without letting you know I was leaving. I wish I could stay cuddled up to you all night but I need to get home to Dog."

Cuddled up to me? Were we cuddling? I vaguely remember laying my head down on his lap. Damnit. We were cuddling.

"You mean Charlie."

"I can't leave him alone all night no matter how much I want to stay here with you."

I nod but keep my mouth shut before I can confess I want him to stay here with me, too. I don't want him to ever leave. Damn it. So much for scratching him off the list of men I love.

Can't he be an asshole for a minute or two? But no, he has to bring me a Christmas gift – a thoughtful Christmas gift – and sit with me all evening because he knows how much it hurts when my parents ignore me on the holidays.

"I can go get Charlie and come back."

"No. No. It's okay. I'm going to bed now anyway. Early day tomorrow."

He studies me for a moment before nodding. "Okay." He kisses my forehead.

I wait until I can no longer hear his footsteps before I bury my head under my blanket and groan. Ugh! What am I going to do about him?

Chapter 12

My feet are dragging as I enter the diner the next day. Unfortunately, the wine and cookies that tasted great yesterday are causing a headache and stomachache today. It's going to be a long day.

I set my purse and coat in my office but before I can get back to work on the kitchen, there's a knock on the door. I frown when I notice Riley waiting for me at the front door.

"You should really give me a key," he says as he storms past me toward the kitchen.

"What are you doing here?" I ask as I follow him.

"Duh. I'm your handyman. And you hired me to help you renovate the diner."

I wring my hands together. I hate to appear weak in front of him, but I can't lie either. "But I can't pay you for your work this week."

I'll have more money after the first of the year, but right now? I'm flat broke.

He shrugs. "You can pay me when you have the money."

"I don't want to owe you."

"What's the big deal? I know you're good for it."

I throw my arms in the air. "No, you don't!"

He steps closer and bends over until our eyes meet. "Of course, I know you're good for it. I know everything about you. Including how you hate to owe anyone. Which means you'll work that fine ass of yours off until you can pay me back. You're the very definition of a low risk investment."

"Are you kidding me?" I hiss at him. "I'm the most high risk investment you can imagine."

He leans back and crosses his arms over his chest. "Why? Give me one reason why you're a risk. And make it a good one."

"Because I've never managed a business before. I have no idea what I'm doing." I motion to the mess around us. "Look at this. If I had been smart, I would have ordered an inspection before I bought this place and then I would have known how much extra work and cost it was. I could have budgeted for it."

He barks out a laugh. What the hell? I open my heart to him and he laughs. What a jerk.

"I really want to slap you again," I grumble.

His laughter cuts off. "I'm not making fun of you."

I raise my eyebrows. "I'm pretty sure laughing at me is the definition of making fun of me."

"I'm sorry. I'm not laughing at you. I'm laughing at the idea of anyone knowing what kind of work they'll end up needing to do when they renovate a building. Especially a building housing a restaurant business."

Now, I'm confused. "What are you saying?"

He lays a hand on my cheek and I want to rub myself against his palm like I'm a cat. *Focus, Moon! We're in the middle of an argument here.*

"I'm saying inspectors don't open walls to check if the pipes are worn. They don't dig through the floors to make sure the foundation isn't settling. And they certainly don't examine the kitchen appliances for wear and tear. Don't you ever watch those renovation shows on television?"

I shake my head.

"Of course, you don't. You'll watch a movie a thousand times—"

"I don't watch movies a thousand times," I interrupt to say.

"But you don't enjoy television shows."

Okay, seriously, who was the woman who had a relationship with this man for a week? I don't tell a man everything about me and reveal all of my secrets after months, let alone days. Except with Riley, I did. Which is why it hurt worse than hell when he ghosted me. Well, that and how much I loved him.

My mother should have warned me about men like him. Men who make you fall in love with them at one look. But my mother wasn't here. She never is.

Riley palms my neck. "What happened? Where did you go?"

I pretend to search the diner. "Um, dude, hate to break it to you but there's no fireplace in here making it impossible to use the floo network."

He chuckles. "You and your love of Harry Potter."

"Ha! You knew what the floo network is so you're a fan, too."

His cheeks darken. "I may have read the books since we met."

"You what?" I sputter. He did not say he's read Harry Potter. He couldn't have.

"Whenever you discuss anything Harry Potter related, your eyes light up and your body vibrates with excitement. Anything that makes you excited is something I want to know about."

How am I supposed to respond to him being this sweet? He's the asshole who ghosted me. He's not supposed to be Mr. Charming. Oh wait. He is Mr. Charming. It's all an act. He can charm my pants off, but he won't stay.

I push him away. "If you're here to work—"

"I am."

"Then, we should get to it."

We're still working on clearing out the kitchen. As we remove the tiles and cupboards, I try not to think about how I thought I could modernize this kitchen without totally replacing every single thing in here. Dwelling on my bleeding funds will not help things.

"You ready to help me remove the sink?" Riley asks.

I glance over at the sink. It's one of those big industrial ones. I hope he doesn't think I can carry it.

"Um, sure. What do I need to do?"

"I've already disconnected the water supply lines, I'm going to disconnect the drainpipe now."

I nod. I'm following him thus far. Thank you, YouTube!

"Can you get some old towels and be ready in case there's any spillage?"

"Got it."

By the time I've gathered up the towels, Riley is on his knees in front of the sink. I freeze at the sight of his ass up in the air. Unlike the plumber cliché, he's not showing any butt crack. What he's showing is a magnificent example of what a man's ass should look like. Seriously, his ass should be displayed on billboards.

And now he's on his knees. A memory of him on his knees in front of me as he lifted my leg and threw it over his shoulder before he ran his nose along my thigh up to my—

"Moon," Riley calls and I force those memories out of my mind before I tackle him.

The man is a god with his mouth. I'd be a fool to not want a repeat. Wait. No. I'd be a fool to want a repeat. Because he's a leaver. Leavers aren't any good. They break your heart.

"What?"

"You okay?"

"I'm fine." My words come out squeaky. I clear my voice and try again. "I'm fine."

He studies me for a second before nodding. "Can you come kneel next to me?"

I maneuver myself until we're shoulder to shoulder.

"I'm going to disconnect the pipe now. There's a chance water spills out. Can you mop it up?"

I hold up my towels. "Sergeant Mopper is ready and waiting."

He grins and mutters, "nut case," under his breath.

He places the pliers around the pipe and tugs. All my attention focuses on his biceps as they strain to open the pipe. I know Riley's strong – lifting me in his arms for wall sex is no easy feat

– but watching those muscles in action? Oh my. Who knew observing a handyman could be such a turn on?

I lift my hand to fan myself and water flies into my face. What the hell? I need cooling off but this is ridiculous. I slap at the water but it keeps on coming.

"Use the towels!" Riley shouts.

"Oh right. The towels."

I grab a towel before crawling under the sink. I retch when the smell of stale water hits me. Gross! I throw the towels down and retreat.

"It stinks!" I say as I heave for fresh breath.

"I didn't realize you're sensitive to smells."

I roll my eyes. "Just because I don't have a gag reflex doesn't mean I don't gag."

Heat flares in his eyes. His hand reaches out for me but before he can touch me, the front door bangs open.

"You-hoo! Is anyone here?"

Clove doesn't wait for a response. She looks around the place until she finds me and Riley sitting on the floor in the kitchen. I don't know what expression I'm wearing, but Riley looks like he's about to tear my clothes off.

Damn busybody. If she hadn't arrived, I'd be naked right now.

"Project Do Over is going to be the easiest money I've ever made."

Her words work better than a cold water shower to remind me why I shouldn't be naked with Riley right now. Do Over. As in the first time was a failure because Riley ghosted me.

I push to my feet. "What are you doing here? Besides spying on us."

She holds up two coffee mugs. "I brought you coffee."

"Thanks," I say as I accept one of the mugs. I nearly smile when I notice Feather peering through the diner window. "What's Feather doing?"

Clove huffs. "Today's my day. Not Feather's." She whirls around and marches off toward the window. Feather sees her coming and scurries away.

"What's Project Do Over?" Riley asks once Clove's gone.

I groan. "You don't want to know."

He ignores my answer. "Because if it means a second chance with you, I'm all for it."

I glare at him. "Don't you have a sink to remove?"

He studies me for a long moment before sighing. "It's okay. You're not there yet. Don't worry. I'll be ready and waiting for you when you are."

"Don't hold your breath," I grumble as I wander off to find something to do away from him because I'm weak where he's concerned. Entirely too weak.

What's stronger than a metal cage? Because the metal cage encasing my heart is too damn frail to keep Riley out. I need something stronger. Much, much stronger.

Chapter 13

RILEY

"Why are we here?" I ask my brothers as I scan the area. We're standing next to a river about a ten-minute hike from the town of Winter Falls.

"Maybe we're going hunting," Miller suggests.

Peace growls. "We don't hunt."

"Why not?" Elder asks.

"Maybe he's afraid to hunt," Miller says.

Elder elbows him. "His name is Peace after all."

Miller snorts. "He wasn't too peaceful when Brody gave Riley a cat for Christmas."

Peace runs a hand through his hair. "Are they always like this?" he asks me.

"Like what?" I ask.

"Like finishing each other's thoughts?" Brody asks.

"Or do you mean annoying?" I ask.

"They're plenty annoying," Brody says.

Peace grunts. "Do all of you do this obnoxious finishing each other sentences thing?"

"Damon doesn't," I say.

"Because he isn't an awesome twin the way we are," Brody adds.

"Twin powers activate!" we shout in unison as we bump fists.

"Why did I think I wanted siblings?" Peace mutters.

"Duh. Because we're awesome," Elder answers.

"Awesome squared!" Brody mimics an explosion with his hands.

"I'm relieved my mom didn't get the Bragg twin gene," Peace grumbles.

"Time for a lesson," I begin.

Brody groans. "Here we go again."

"Having identical twins isn't genetic."

Brody grins. "It's just lucky."

I ignore him. "But fraternal twins." I point to Miller and Elder who might look alike but aren't identical the way Brody and I are. "Do run in the family. But the gene is from the mother's family. Not the father's."

"I prefer to have as few genes from dear old dad as possible," Miller mumbles, and I nod in agreement.

"I'm supposed to be the one giving lessons today," Peace says.

Brody groans. "Oh no. He thinks he's the big brother since Damon took off."

"If you're going to lecture us, I'm going back to bed," Miller grumbles before turning toward town.

"Hold on," Peace orders.

"Oh no. He used his cop voice. We're in trouble," Elder sings.

"Maybe he's going to kill us and throw us in the water. This is so exciting." Brody rubs his hands together.

Peace glares at him. "You're excited about me killing you?"

"Ha!" Brody points at him. "He admitted it."

"Is he always like this?" Peace asks me.

"Did you forget about cat-pocalypse on Christmas already?"

Elder steps close to Peace to study him. "Maybe he's been hit in the head too many times."

Peace elbows Elder. "I wasn't hit in the head too many times."

"Or maybe whipped too many times by Olivia." Brody pretends to crack a whip. "Whup-ah!"

"What does being whipped have to do with forgetfulness?" I ask.

Brody shrugs. "Nothing. But how else could I bring up how Peace is whipped?"

I roll my eyes. "As if you don't want a woman who loves you the way Olivia loves Peace."

Peace rocks back on his heels and smiles. "She does love me."

"Is this the part where you discuss sex? I'm out." Miller attempts to flee again.

"No, this is the male bonding ritual." Peace's words have Miller freezing again.

Brody bounces on his toes. "There's a male bonding ritual? Why didn't anyone tell me? Is it secret? Do we have to take blood oaths? Did someone bring a knife?"

"How do you put up with him?" Peace asks.

"He's like a blue cheese. Stinky but once you get used to the smell, it's not completely revolting," Elder explains.

"You want to see my blue cheese?" Brody toes off his boot.

"If Brody's stripping, I'm out of here." Miller marches for the tree line.

"Brody's not the only one who's stripping."

Peace's words have Miller turning around. "What?"

Brody doesn't wait for an explanation before removing his jacket and throwing it on the ground where his boots already are. "Full Monty or do we leave our tighty whities on?" he asks as he removes his sweatshirt.

Miller's brow furrows. "I did not come out here to see my brother's dick."

"Why not? Are you afraid you don't measure up?" Brody thrusts his hips.

"I'll show you." Miller unbuttons his jeans and shoves them down his legs.

"Someone's not wearing tighty whities," Elder mumbles when Miller's dick is revealed.

"This is not a dick measuring contest," Peace says.

"It's not?" Brody holds up his phone. "Then, why am I downloading a tape measure app?"

"Oh please. I bet you already had the app downloaded," I say.

"Not all of us are handymen who carry a tape measure around with them."

"Not all of us feel the need to measure our dicks." I waggle my eyebrows. "I know how big mine is."

"The question is – does Moon know?"

I glare at my twin. He knows all about my relationship with Moon, but he's just mad because I haven't filled him in on my progress since we've been in Winter Falls. Twins are nosy as hell.

"I should have drowned you in the bathtub when we were children."

He spreads his arms wide. "And miss out on all this awesomeness?"

"Wouldn't that be a shame," Miller mumbles.

I latch onto the chance to change the subject. "Why are you still standing there with your dick hanging out?"

He shrugs. "Peace told us to get naked."

"Dude, you're wearing your jacket and gloves but no pants. You're not naked."

"It gets the job done."

"What job?" Elder asks. "The only job you want to do with your dick is named Eden and she won't give you the time of day."

"I don't want Eden," Miller denies.

"It's cute how you think you can lie to your twin."

"We don't have superpowers."

"No twin superpowers. Check." Peace claps his hands. "Moving on. It's time to swim."

I cock my eyebrow. "Swim? You do know it's December."

"Don't worry. The water is freezing cold no matter what time of year you get into it. It's why the town is named Winter Falls after all."

"Thanks for the history lesson, but I'm not getting in some freezing cold water for some male bonding ritual bullshit."

Uh oh. Miller should know better than to provoke Elder and Brody by now.

"Are you afraid your tiny wiener is going to freeze off?" Elder taunts.

Miller punches his hips. "Pretty sure I showed all of you my dick is not small."

He shouldn't have let himself be distracted. Brody plows into him. When he starts to fall, Brody grabs his legs while Elder takes his arms. Together they carry him toward the river.

"Assholes! At least let me save my wallet and keys."

I hold up the objects. "You mean these."

Miller opens his mouth to yell at me but Brody and Elder begin the countdown.

"One, two," they shout as they swing Miller back and forth between them. "Two and a half, three!"

Miller flies through the air before splashing into the water.

"Run!" Brody yells.

Not happening. I block him before he can make it two steps. "You can't stop me."

"Sure we can," Elder says before tackling Brody. I grab his arms and together Elder and I throw Brody into the water.

"I hate this family!" he shouts as he flies through the air.

"I knew having brothers would be fun," Peace says as he strips. He races for the river and jumps in.

"Come on, charmer!" Brody tries to splash me. "Get in here."

I don't bother fighting him. I know there's zero chance of me not getting into the water. Either I can get thrown in or I can jump in myself. The choice is easy. I strip my clothes off and dive into the water. Elder isn't far behind me.

"Holy crap! This water is freezing." I shiver.

Peace chuckles. "Which is why we try not to get our hair wet."

It's like he's waving a red flag at a bunch of horny bulls. He really didn't grow up with brothers. I splash him to distract him while Brody ducks under the water and swims behind him. Brody pops up behind Peace and shoves his head under the water.

"Asshole," Peace sputters when he manages to make it to the surface. He splashes Brody and soon enough all of us have wet hair and are freezing. No one complains when I climb out of the water to the river bank. They all follow me instead.

"Does this mean you've come to terms with having another family?" I ask Peace once we're dressed and making our way back to town for some coffee to warm up.

"Do I have a choice? Mom's adopted you lot of hooligans and all you losers now live in town."

I bump his shoulder. "Ah, you love us."

"The way you love Moon?"

I hold up my fist for him to bump. "Dude, you've got this brother thing nailed."

Brody wraps an arm around my neck. "No avoidance. What's the plan to win Moon back?"

"There is no plan."

"You're an idiot." He rubs his knuckles over my hair and I shove him away. "And you're a liar."

He's not wrong. I did lie. I do have a plan. Moon doesn't need some grand gesture or fancy presents. She wants someone who shows up every single day for her, which is exactly what I intend to do. I will show up every damn day until she gives me another chance. I'll break her down eventually.

Chapter 14

WHEN I HEAR THE music blaring from inside of *Electric Vibes*, I groan. It's New Year's Eve, but I have no desire to party. My muscles are sore from the manual labor of renovating the diner all week. And who knew resisting temptation in the form of the sexiest handyman to ever walk the earth is this tiring? Trust me. It is.

"Why are you dillydallying?" Ashlyn asks when she notices I'm dragging my feet.

"Did Rowan buy you a dictionary of fifties vocabulary words for Christmas?"

"Don't be silly. The word dillydally is much older than the fifties."

"In other words, Aspen bought you another dictionary for Christmas."

"I don't know what my oldest sister's problem is. She acts like I don't know what words mean."

"Probably because you make up definitions all the time."

She sniffs and lifts her nose in the air. "Incorrect. I make words better all the time."

"Ashlyn my way or the highway dragged you out, too?" Harmony asks as she joins us on the sidewalk in front of the bar.

"It's New Year's Eve!" Ashlyn shouts. "No dragging should be involved. Unless it's by the hair."

I hold up my hands. "Whoa. Too much information, Ashlyn Bashlyn."

She wiggles her eyebrows. "Tell me you don't want Riley to pull your hair."

"I don't want Riley to pull my hair."

Do I want him to pull other things? Maybe. Okay. Yes. I do. But it's not happening. No matter how sexy he is walking around with a toolbelt around his waist. I've sunk to new lows. I now find toolbelts sexy.

"She's lying," Soleil says as she and Eden stop next to us.

"Yeah! The gang's all here." Ashlyn laces her arm through mine. "Let's get this party started."

When we go inside, we're greeted by Cassandra's fiancé who's standing at the entrance holding a tray of drinks.

"On the house," Cedar says as he hands us each a martini glass.

"What is it?" I ask.

"Who cares?" Ashlyn takes a sip. "Yum. Citrussy. Thanks brother-in-law."

"It's a clementine martini," Cedar explains.

"How did Cassie convince you to come out tonight?" Ashlyn asks.

He wiggles his eyebrows.

I walk away. I have zero interest in listening to someone else brag about their sex life since mine is now non-existent. Unless you count playing with my vibrator, which I don't.

Judging by how packed *Electric Vibes* is, the entire town is here. Including the gossip gals. Tonight they're wearing bright pink tank tops with the words *New Year, Same Me, Lucky You!* on them. Despite myself, I giggle.

"All right all you groovy dudes and dudettes. It's time for New Year's Eve karaoke," Lennon announces from the stage. "First up, Moon Star."

"I didn't put my name in," I shout at him.

"Thank goodness. Someone doesn't know what pitch is."

I glance to the side to find out who spoke. Love Hill. Maneater, man stealer, and overall mean girl of Winter Falls. I avoid her as best I can. I don't want to be in her crosshairs. Ashlyn's sister, Aspen, got in her crosshairs once and it nearly destroyed her relationship with Lyric. The two are married now, but they lost over a decade together due to Love Hill's antics.

I shiver and look away. My gaze lands on the gaggle of gossip gals motioning me toward the stage. Guess I don't need to wonder who volunteered for me to sing karaoke first anymore.

"Get up here, Moon. Or are you chicken?" Lennon taunts.

I am not a chicken! I finish my martini and slam the glass down on the nearest table before marching to the stage. I jump on it and snatch the microphone.

"Bring it on."

I got this. Except when I see what song's teed up on the monitor, I realize I don't got this.

"This is a duet."

"Oh really?" Sage widens her eyes as if she's innocent. She hasn't been innocent since the day she took the job as police dispatcher and promptly began using all the information she heard there to begin her bookie business. "I didn't realize."

"Who helped her pick out this song?" I ask the crowd because there's no way any of the gossip gals know this song.

Ashlyn waves from in front of the stage. "You'll thank me later."

The crowd parts for Riley as he saunters toward the stage. "I'm told my presence is requested."

I narrow my eyes on him. "By whom?"

He doesn't have a chance to respond before the music to *Need You Now* by Lady Antebellum begins. He climbs onto the stage and stands next to me. I try to step back but he shakes his head.

"We need to share the microphone."

Damn. Good point.

"Can you even sing?"

He smirks. "I guess we're about to find out." He elbows me. "You're up."

I glance away from him and concentrate on the lyrics on the monitor despite having the words memorized. My voice wobbles as I sing the first few verses.

Riley squeezes my waist and I relax. No matter what our relationship status is, having him near makes me feel safe and protected. Damn him.

When it's his turn to sing, I try to hand the microphone to him, but he leans close to me instead. He starts to sing and my knees go weak. His voice is deep and raspy. It makes me think of sex and sweaty sheets.

He nudges me when the chorus comes – oops! I may have gotten lost in his voice for a second there – and we sing together with our cheeks touching. His breath on my hand holding the mic causes warmth to spread through me until my core's on fire. My eyes fall closed and I let myself enjoy his voice as he sings.

I pretend he means the words. How he needs me. How he misses me.

Applause erupts and I startle. I forgot we're not alone. We're in a crowded bar on New Year's Eve. A crowd now holding their phones above them with the lighter app on as they sway from side to side.

"Encore! Encore!" Ashlyn shouts and stomps her feet.

Her husband sighs. "Dream girl."

"What? It's New Year's Eve. I'm allowed to get rowdy. It's written in our prenup."

"There's nothing about New Year's Eve in our prenup."

"No? I'll have my lawyer contact your lawyer."

Rowan shakes his head as if he's annoyed with his wife but the smile on his lips and the warmth in his eyes tell another story. He'd do anything for Ashlyn. There's a reason he calls her his dream girl after all.

I want what they have. I want someone to love me with the same fierceness. I want someone who will do anything for me. But, mostly, I want someone who stays. Someone who doesn't abandon me. Someone who doesn't ghost me.

I clear my throat and hand Riley the microphone before rushing off the stage toward the women's restroom.

"I don't know what Riley sees in her," I freeze when I hear Love Hill's voice before I can enter the restroom. "She's plain. And have you seen her hands?"

I glance down at my hands. My nail polish is long gone. Worst yet? My fingernails are doing a fabulous impression of a woman who's never seen the inside of a nail salon. And there are callouses forming on my palms. To top it all off, the cut I got a few weeks ago still isn't healed.

"He'll be easy prey for me."

At her words, rage fills me. She is not stealing Riley away from me. I hit the restroom door and it flies open.

"It's about time someone brings you down a peg."

She peers down her nose at me. "And you think you're qualified?" She sniffs.

"I've just accepted the job."

My hands are balled into fists at my side. I could deck her. Right here. Right now. But I really do hate the idea of spending a night in jail.

"You are out of your league with Riley Bragg. A man like him will never stay with you."

Fuck not spending a night in jail. I raise my fist and swing at her, but before I can connect with her obnoxiously pretty face, Riley catches my arm and drags me away. I fight his hold.

"Let me go. I've got a score to settle with the skank."

"Just because every man in Winter Falls wants to have sex with me doesn't mean I'm a skank."

"Bitch. Having sex with every man in town who has a heartbeat is the very definition of skank," I shout at her.

Riley lifts me up and throws me over his shoulder. I pound my fists on his back.

"Let me down! I'm going to tear her botoxed lips off of her face."

He opens a door and slams it shut behind us. When he sets me down, I rush for the exit but he maneuvers me until my back is up against the wall and he's plastered to my front. I can feel how hard he is.

"Do fighting women turn you on?"

Riley smirks. "You were jealous."

I glance away. "Whatever."

He pinches my chin and uses the hold to force me to meet his gaze. "It was sexy as hell witnessing you fight for me."

"I wasn't fighting for you. I was fighting Love Hill because she's a bitch."

He brushes my hair off my forehead and my eyes fall closed. He's too close to me. His wood and oil scent surrounds me. I should walk away. This is dangerous. But then his lips brush lightly over my forehead before he trails kisses down my face. And I realize I'm not going anywhere. Because I'm done fighting.

"Let's go. I'm done fighting you."

Chapter 15

RILEY

"I'm done fighting you."

My heart stops at Moon's words. Finally. She's giving me a second chance.

I frame her face with my hands. "You sure?"

"Let's go before I change my mind."

I stay where I am. "You didn't say yes."

She pushes up on her toes until her eyes are level with mine and grabs my ears. "How's this for yes? Please take me to your home, get me naked, and do wicked, wicked things to me."

My cock nearly jumps out of my pants. He is on board with getting naked right here, right now. I moan and crash my lips down on hers. She sighs and I slip my tongue inside. She tastes of strawberry and sunshine and I can't get enough. I want to drown in her scent.

Her hands thread through my hair and she pulls me near until I can feel her breasts straining against my chest. I thrust my hips forward until my hard length rubs against her and she moans. I catch her leg and throw it around my waist.

The door bangs open and I wrench my lips from Moon's.

Cassandra's eyes widen before she glances over her shoulder and shouts, "You knew they were in here, didn't you?"

"Are their clothes on?"

"Are their lips locked?"

"What base are they on?"

"Kissing but clothes are still on," Cassie answers.

"Traitor," Moon mutters as she drops her leg.

Cassie snorts. "You would have done the exact same thing."

Moon sniffs. "I would not have invaded your privacy."

"Liar. You would have snuck in here first before going out there and starting the betting with a distinct advantage."

"Whatever."

"I'll hold them back if you want to sneak out the rear entrance."

Moon grabs my hand. "Come on. We need to hurry."

"Hurry? What's going on?"

She doesn't answer as she leads me out the door to the hallway where a crowd has gathered.

"Do I see the gossip gals?" I ask when I notice the bright pink sweatshirts.

Cassie giggles. "Welcome to Winter Falls."

We rush down the hallway and out the door into the night. "Your house or mine?"

"Um…" My mind is still trying to catch up.

"Never mind. Your house. Charlie can't be left alone."

"Is voyeurism a thing in this town?" I ask once we're walking in the right direction.

"What?" Her nose wrinkles. "No! I mean there are some people who would watch if we gave them a show, but it's not an actual thing."

"Then, what was going on back there?"

"Back there where? And why are you walking this slow?"

I smirk. "Are you in a hurry?"

"I haven't had a non-self-induced orgasm in three months."

Three months? Three months was the last time we were together.

"You haven't been with anyone since me?"

She stops and whirls around to glare at me. "And you have? It's barely been three months."

I palm her neck and haul her near. "I haven't been with anyone since you. You're the only one I want."

She opens her mouth to say something but snaps it closed again. I know what she's thinking, but I don't want to discuss why I ghosted her now. I don't ever want to discuss why I hurt her. I'm going to have to come clean at some point but not when my cock is hard enough to replace the hammer in my toolbelt.

"You're the only woman I want spread out naked in front of me."

She blows out a breath. "Okay. Let's do this," she says and resumes her march toward my house.

We reach my house within minutes since it's mere blocks from the bar. Nothing is far away in this small town. Moon bounces up the stairs and nearly slams into the door when she pushes on it and it doesn't open.

"What's going on? Why is your door locked? Never mind." She motions to the lock. "Open sesame."

As soon as we're inside, I gather her in my arms and hurry up the stairs to the bedroom.

"Someone's got ants in his pants."

"Oh baby, I've got something in my pants, but it's not ants."

She giggles and I mold my lips to hers to capture her happiness. She rubs her hand over my jeans until I can feel moisture gather at the tip of my cock. I lay her down on the bed before crawling on top of her.

"Yes," she hisses as I trail kisses along her jaw to her ear.

"Yes, what?" I whisper in her ear before biting on her lobe. She grinds her pelvis into me and I realize we're wearing entirely too many clothes.

I kneel and grasp the hem of her sweater. "Time for this to go."

She raises her arms and I pull the material over her head revealing her sexy lace bra.

"I remember this," I murmur as I trail my finger along the edge of the lace.

"I didn't plan this. I didn't have any other clean bras."

I wish she had planned this. I wish she wanted to give me a second chance as much as I want one. But it doesn't matter now. She's here in my bed where she belongs. Where she should always be.

"Are you going to move anytime soon?"

Nope. I'm savoring the moment the woman I love is finally back with me. But I keep those thoughts to myself. Moon will flee this house as fast as she can if I voice my love for her now.

"Impatient?"

She knifes up and captures my cock in her hand. "I'm not the only one," she says as she squeezes.

I groan and my head falls backward as she unzips my jeans and pulls me out. She swipes a finger over the tip and I nearly come. "Fuck."

"That's what we're doing," she sings before her mouth swallows me.

My eyes fly open to watch her bob up and down on my cock. I gather the silky strands of her hair in my hands. Her eyes sparkle as she looks up at me. She knows I never last long when she gets her mouth on me. She thinks she's getting her way. I don't fucking care. I'll make sure we're both satisfied before this night is over. More than one time if I have my way.

She cradles my balls in her hands and I growl. "Enough!"

When she continues to suck, I use my hold on her hair to pull her off me. "Clothes off now."

She giggles as she falls on her back. She kicks off her boots before shimmying out of her jeans and panties. When she reaches behind her to remove her bra, I stop her. "The bra stays."

She lays back on the bed and raises her hands above her head causing her breasts to thrust forward.

"You little minx," I grumble as I remove my t-shirt. I don't bother with my jeans. I'll get rid of them for round two.

I line my cock up at her entrance. "You still on the pill?" She nods. "You okay with me taking you bare?"

I hope to hell so because nothing feels better than Moon's walls surrounding me without a layer of latex separating us.

She wraps her legs around me. "Hurry up."

I don't move. I won't enter her until she gives me the green light.

"What do you want me to say? Please take me, you big stallion. I can't wait to feel your throbbing member inside of me."

I chuckle. "Say you're okay with me taking you bare."

She lifts three fingers in a girl scout salute. "On my honor, I solemnly swear I am more than okay with you taking me bare."

I slam into her and she arches her back as she moans. "Holy cow. I forgot how big you are."

I freeze. "You okay."

She punches my shoulder. "I am but you won't be if you don't start moving."

I slowly withdraw as her walls clench around me. "Fuck."

"Don't just say it. Do it," she says as she squeezes her inner muscles.

"Is this what you want?" I demand as I thrust into her over and over again.

"Hell yeah."

Pfft.

I freeze. "Did you…?"

She slaps me. "Farting is completely normal, but it wasn't me."

"It wasn't me."

Pfft.

I glance over my shoulder. Charlie is standing at the end of the bed staring at us as he farts away.

"Oh no. Farty dog is here." Moon giggles.

"Is he judging us?"

"I don't think your dog is going to hold up a scoreboard. Nine for thrust technique. Eight for finger skill."

I swirl my hips and she moans. "A nine for thrust technique?"

I pull out to the tip before slamming into her. The bed squeaks as it rocks forward until the headboard hits the wall.

"A nine?"

"The dog," she breathes out.

"Can watch for all I care."

I reach in between us to find her clit. "An eight for finger skill?"

"Show me whatcha got big guy."

I pinch her clit. Her walls flutter around me and her eyes fall closed. I pinch it again as I plunge into her. Her walls squeeze me.

"Not yet."

Her eyes fly open. "I'll come when I want to come."

"Fucking stubborn woman."

Her nails dig into my shoulders as I thrust into her again and again until I find my rhythm. My balls tighten.

"Now you can come," I say as I pinch her clit one last time.

"Riley," she breathes out as her walls clamp down on me and she climaxes.

I'm right behind her. "Moonbeam, I…"

I manage to shut my mouth before I declare my love to her during sex.

"That was awesome," I say before I collapse.

Pfft.

Moon giggles. "I think farty dog agrees."

Chapter 16

RILEY

I smile at the scent of cinnamon and sugar wafting from my pillow. Moon always smells like she's been baking all day. I reach out for her but my eyes fly open when I only encounter cold, empty space on the other side of the bed.

"Moon?"

Charlie barks in response. I sit up in bed and rub my hand down my face.

"Where is she, boy?"

He howls.

"Did she fucking run away?"

I jump out of bed to search for her. Five minutes later it's confirmed. She's gone and there's no note.

"Maybe she went to buy us breakfast?"

I swear Charlie looks at me with pity.

"Except it's New Year's Day and all the stores and restaurants in Winter Falls are closed."

What the hell is she thinking?

Pfft.

"I agree, buddy. It's shit."

I rush back upstairs to find my clothes. As soon as I'm dressed, I'll be paying Moon a visit. Run away from me, will she? I don't think so.

I open my door and nearly bump into my twin.

"What are you doing here?" I ask Brody.

"It's Hogmanay."

"What?" I push past him. "I don't have time for your pranks right now. I need to find Moon." I start walking toward her house. Brody follows me.

"Find Moon? Did you lose her? I thought you'd be putting your banana in her fruit salad by now."

"Why are you here if you thought I'd be with Moon?"

"I told you. Hogmanay. We need to be the first footers."

"And I told you. No pranks today."

"Hogmanay isn't a prank. It's a tradition here in Winter Falls."

We pass Elder's house and he runs out with Miller on his heels. "Wait up!"

I stop. "Someone needs to explain what's going on because I don't have time for your hints and jokes."

"It's Hogmanay," Elder says.

"Saying a made up word doesn't explain shit."

"Hogmanay isn't made up," he says.

"It's a new year's tradition in Scotland," Brody says.

"Do I need to remind everyone we're not in Scotland?"

"It dates back to pagan times," Elder says.

"And Winter Falls loves pagan traditions," Miller adds.

"If we want to be the first footers, we need to hurry. Do you have your offerings?" Brody holds up a bag.

"I don't know what a first footer is. I don't have any offerings. And I'm not going anywhere with you lot." I march off in the direction of Moon's house again. They've held me up enough for today.

Miller's hand lands on my shoulder. "Wait."

"We're going to Clementine and Eagle's first," Elder says.

"You have fun there." I try to leave but Miller's hand clamps down.

"You're coming with us. It's a family tradition and Peace invited us."

I sigh at Elder's explanation. I can't skip family traditions. But I'm not giving up quite yet.

"But I don't have any offerings."

Brody waves his bag in my face. "No worries. I got the best Bragg twins covered."

Crap. "Fine. Let's go get this over with."

We travel in the opposite direction of Moon's house to where Peace's parents live.

"What are the offerings anyway?" I ask as we walk.

"Dark rye bread and a lump of coal," Elder says.

I cock an eyebrow. "Are you serious? This isn't one of your jokes?"

"Nope. Dark rye bread – aka a black bun – is to ensure the people you visit don't go hungry in the year ahead and the lump of coal is to ensure the house remains warm in the coming months," he explains.

"And everyone shows up at their family's house to give them these gifts?"

At his nod, an idea begins to form in my mind. All I have to do is find some rye bread and a lump of coal. I eye Brody's bag. No, forget Brody's bag. I'll steal Miller's. He's the safe bet.

"And what's a first footer?"

"Hopefully us," Brody says as he bounds up the stairs to the front door of Peace's parent's house. "Hello!" he shouts as he pounds on it.

Clementine opens the door. "You're early."

"Because I wanted to be the first footer to arrive." He hands her the bag. "Happy Hogmanay!"

"Come in." She ushers us inside.

We gather in the living room where Eagle is waiting. "Happy Hogmanay," he greets.

"Peace and Olivia aren't here?" When Eagle shakes his head, Brody pumps his fist. "Awesome! First Hogmanay in Winter Falls and I'm winning!"

"What's this?" Clementine asks as she opens the bag Brody gave her.

"Bread and coal."

"This isn't coal." She holds up a block of wood.

"Guess someone isn't winning now," Elder whispers to me.

Brody shrugs. "I painted it black."

I frown. "Please tell me you didn't steal the paint from my woodworking shop."

He doesn't bother attempting to sound truthful when he says, "I didn't steal the paint from your woodworking shop."

"Liar. If you left a mess, you're cleaning it up."

"You always make such a big deal about a little paint on the floor."

I groan. "You tipped over an entire container of paint, didn't you?"

He motions toward the bag he gave Clementine. "Check what else is in there."

She removes a plastic bag. "A sandwich."

"The plastic bag is one of those reusable ones, so no hauling me over the coals." He wiggles his eyebrows. "Get it? Coals."

"Hey!" Elder elbows him. "I'm the jokester in the family. Speaking of which, what does a loaf of bread say to a friend after doing them a favor? It's the yeast I can do. Get it? Yeast."

Brody moans. "Dad jokes? It's too early in the morning for dad jokes."

"I thought you were supposed to bring rye bread," I say as I indicate the sandwich.

"Rye bread is gross. Besides, I figured someone might get hungry."

"Does anyone want a sandwich?" Clementine asks.

"I can eat." Miller can always eat.

She hands him the sandwich and he unwraps it before biting into it.

"Oh no!" She gestures toward the sandwich. "It's moldy."

Miller holds it up to the light and studies it before stuffing it back in his mouth.

Clementine snatches it away. "You are not eating a moldy sandwich. We have food."

"It's not mold," Miller mumbles between bites.

She points out the green and blue spots on the bread. "Yes, it is. I can see it…" Her voice trails off and she frowns. "Is this food coloring?"

Brody claps. "Fooled you, though, didn't I?"

"I swear no one dropped him on his head when he was a baby. He feels obliged to be this way because he's the youngest," I explain.

He rolls his eyes. "I'm less than two minutes younger than you."

"Two minutes to travel the birth canal? In addition to being older than you, I'm way faster."

"I'll race you right now." He pumps his arms as if to warm up. He can warm up all he wants. I'm faster than the geek who spends all of his time behind a computer.

"Where to?"

"Boys!" Eagle shouts and we freeze. "No one's racing."

"We aren't?" Peace asks as he arrives with Olivia. "I'm the fastest."

"That's what she said," Elder mumbles and Brody gives him a high-five.

"You're late. We're the first footers," Brody teases Peace.

"Because someone isn't the fastest," Olivia says.

Clementine snorts and Olivia backpedals, "I meant with showering." Her cheeks darken and it's obvious what they were doing in the shower this morning. "With getting dressed I mean."

"I think she means with getting undressed." Elder winks and the blush on Olivia's face darkens further.

Peace throws an arm around her shoulders. "Don't worry about Mom. She's a Winter Falls native. She's not afraid to discuss sex."

"Sex is perfectly natural," Clementine says and I groan in unison with my brothers.

"Holy Hogmanay. This is priceless," Olivia says and I glance up from my perusal of the floor.

"What is?"

She indicates my brothers who are all studying the floor.

"The Bragg brothers are embarrassed by a woman discussing sex."

"Not any woman." I wink at her. "I'll talk about sex with you all day long."

"No, you won't," Peace growls.

She pats his chest. "Let him be. A little flirting never hurt anyone."

Peace shakes his head. "You're such a troublemaker."

Speaking of troublemakers, how long do I need to stay here? I eye the front door. Will anyone notice if I slip out?

"Go," Clementine says.

Does she mean me? *Me?* I mouth.

"Yes, you. Go."

"Yeah, dude. You need to make things right with Moon before she poisons your food," Olivia adds.

"What?"

"Everyone knows Moon snuck out of your house in the middle of the night."

Is she serious? "How?" I didn't know until thirty minutes ago when I woke up.

She shrugs. "I don't know. I suspect the gossip gals have surveillance set up around town. Some type of cameras with recording devices. They probably have motion sensors to switch them on. Which is why it's impossible to keep a secret in Winter Falls."

"Unless you're me." Elder puffs out his chest.

Clementine nudges me toward the door. "Don't give her too much time to think."

"Here," Olivia hands me a burlap bag. "You can't arrive empty handed on Hogmanay."

"You're certain?" I ask Clementine as she opens the door for me. "I don't want you to miss out on my charming self on Hogmanay."

"Stop flirting with my wife," Eagle yells.

I lean down to kiss Clementine's cheek. "Have a happy Hogmanay," I say despite still not understanding what the hell Hogmanay is.

Chapter 17

I FREEZE WHEN THERE'S a knock on the door but relax when I notice it's barely one in the afternoon. There's no way Riley's here since he'll still be with his brothers celebrating Hogmanay at this time of day. It must be Ashlyn stopping by on her way to her parent's house.

"Oh, it's you." I frown at Riley.

He lifts up a bag. "Happy Hogmanay!"

Huh. I expected him to show up here all pissed off at me for sneaking out on him. Maybe he doesn't want a second chance after all. Maybe he was merely scratching an itch. And maybe the bag he's holding is one of my own.

"Did you seriously bring me my own black bun?"

"Your own black bun?"

"I make all the black buns for Hogmanay."

Thank the heavens since I need the money. Bad. I'm hoping the huge pile of debtors I have will be satisfied with down payments on my debts because I won't have the money to pay off anyone until I can open the diner. Even once the diner's open it's going to be a struggle for a while.

Riley snags the bun from the bag. "You made this?"

"I told you I did less than a minute ago."

He stuffs the bread into his mouth.

"What are you doing? You're not supposed to eat the gift you brought for me."

His eyes fall closed and he moans. The sound reminds me of how he moans when he's moving inside of me. The memory causes my body to light up and my nipples to stand at attention. I cross my arms over my chest before he can notice how hard my nipples are.

He swallows his bite and grins at me. "This is delicious. The diner's going to be overrun by customers if you make this every day."

Assuming the diner ever opens, I think but don't say because I have no desire to discuss my fears about the business with this man. He knows too many of my secret concerns and worries already.

"Black bun is for Hogmanay only."

He shrugs and takes another bite. "I thought it would be bitter because of the rye bread, but it's actually sweet," he says with his mouth full.

"Rye bread is a misconception because of how dark it appears. It's sweet due to the fruit. There are raisins, currants, and almonds in it."

"It's amazing. I bet it pairs well with coffee."

I roll my eyes. "Smooth move."

He smirks. "Some say I'm a smooth operator."

"Some say you're a dork."

He winks. "About that coffee?"

I open the door and usher him inside. Not like I have a choice when Petal of the gossip gal gang happens to be walking by. And by 'happens' I mean she's been strolling back and forth in front of the house ever since Riley showed up. She's not exactly subtle. She'd probably get kicked out of the gossip gal gang if she tried being discreet.

"You drink whiskey with a black bun. Not coffee."

His nose wrinkles. "Whiskey?"

Honestly, most people drink coffee with their bun, but I happen to know Riley hates whiskey. "We can't ignore tradition."

"No, we can't," he grumbles as he sits at the dining room table while I pour us two drams of whiskey. I might make sure his is extra full because he deserves it.

"Happy Hogmanay!" I shout as I lift my glass.

He makes a face before drinking the whiskey. I'm surprised he doesn't hold his nose. He coughs as he sets the glass down.

"Don't like whiskey?"

His eyes narrow on me. "You know I don't."

I bat my eyelashes. "Maybe I forgot."

"Maybe I don't believe you."

I shrug. Of course, I remember he doesn't like whiskey. It's hard to forget getting thrown out of an Irish pub. It wasn't my first time getting thrown out of a drinking establishment, but it was my first time experiencing the event sober. Who gets thrown out of a bar sober? Riley Bragg, that's who.

"You want to tell me why you snuck out of my house this morning?"

Now, it's my turn to cough. "I'd rather discuss your list of reasons why you hate whiskey."

And there is a list. There's a reason we got kicked out of the bar after all. Riley can't charm his way out of every situation.

"Will you please tell me why you left our bed this morning?"

Our bed. Not hardly.

"I thought we agreed last night we'd explore our relationship further."

"I didn't agree to shit." I didn't. It's not my fault he made assumptions.

"Please."

His hand reaches across the table to grasp mine. I clutch my hands in my lap before I give in to the temptation to touch him. Touching his hand will likely lead to me touching other parts of him. Which will end up with us tearing up the sheets. An idea I find difficult enough to ignore when we're not touching.

"Maybe I wanted to leave you before you could leave me again," I snap to hide how much I want to launch myself over this table and into his arms. "Experience how it felt to be on the other side of the leaving for a change."

"And how did it feel?"

It felt horrible. I could barely tear myself away from his arms. No one's ever held me all night long the way he does. It makes me feel precious. A feeling I know can be addictive. I needed to cut myself off before the addiction set in.

When I finally managed to get out of bed, I snuck down the stairs with Charlie following me the entire way. When I put my shoes on, he cried as if he knew I was leaving. I damn near broke down and cried with the dog.

"I know the day I stopped returning your messages was the worst day of my life. I was literally sick to my stomach."

At the reminder of his abandonment, my stomach sours. "Then, why did you ghost me?"

He drops his chin to study the surface of the table.

"This is why I left your house."

He glances up at me. "This? What this?"

"Your inability to tell me the truth." I shake my head. "No, you're not lying to me. You can't even bother with lying."

His brow wrinkles. "Would you rather I lie to you?"

I throw my arms in the air. "No! But refusing to answer is worse."

He clears his throat. "Will you accept me admitting the reason I ghosted you has nothing to do with you?"

I snort. He must be kidding. I literally told him less than a minute ago refusing to answer is worse than lying. Is he not listening to a word I'm saying?

"No. I will not. How can I trust you not to abandon me again when I don't know the reason why you abandoned me in the first place?"

He flinches. "I didn't abandon you."

"Yes, you did. We were discussing me moving to San Diego to be with you. You said you loved me. How is ghosting me not abandoning me in this scenario?"

And he knows how I feel about being left behind. He knows everything about my parents leaving. Even more than Ashlyn and she was with me here in this very house when it happened.

"Don't you fucking dare compare me to your parents."

I rear back at the venom in his voice. "I wasn't."

"I know when you're thinking of your parents."

I glare at him. "You do not."

"You frown and this vein in your forehead pulses whenever you think of them and get upset."

"Fine. I was thinking of them. But I wasn't comparing you to them."

He glares at me.

"I wasn't," I growl before going in for the kill. "I was thinking what you did was worse than them leaving me. You knew I had abandonment issues and yet you abandoned me anyway. I vote your actions are worse."

"I don't."

"Too bad. You don't get a vote in how Moon feels."

"I want a vote. I want a second chance."

"You know the requirement to being granted a second chance." I stare at him but he doesn't speak. He doesn't tell me why he left me.

"I'm sorry, Moon. I'll give you anything you want in this world, but I can't give you that."

"Too bad an explanation is the only thing I want." I stand. "It's time for you to go."

"I don't want to go anywhere. I want to spend the day with you. We can watch a movie. I won't complain when you talk the whole way through it."

I slam my palms down on the table. "And I want an explanation. Looks like neither one of us is getting what they want today."

I wave toward the door. "Now get out of here before I call your brother to come get you."

"This isn't over," he says as he stands.

"Yeah, it is."

I wait until the door closes behind him before I collapse on the chair. I'll give myself today to mourn the loss of the love of my life. No more. I'm done with his inability to talk to me. If he can't talk to me now, how would our relationship ever survive long term?

Chapter 18

I'm staring at the gutted kitchen in the diner when the door opens and Riley marches inside.

"I'm surprised you showed up," I snap to hide my relief at his arrival. As much as it kills me to admit it, I can't finish this renovation without him.

"I always show up."

I flinch. Except for when it's me apparently.

"Damnit, Moon. I'm sorry." He reaches for me, but I dance out of the way.

"We should get to work. I missed the holiday season, but I want to be open for Imbolc."

"What's Imbolc?"

"Ask your brother."

"I'm asking you."

Yeah, well, maybe I don't feel like answering his questions. Maybe I want him to feel the way I do when he refuses to answer my questions.

I dig the envelope of money out of my back pocket and offer it to him. "Here."

He doesn't accept it. "What's this?"

I wave the envelope at him. "It's not everything I owe you."

He frowns. "I told you, you don't have to pay me for working last week."

Yeah, I do. I don't accept favors. Especially not from him.

"I owe you for December."

He rubs a hand over his beard. "I haven't sent you an invoice yet."

I raise my eyebrows. "Were you planning on sending me an invoice?"

"Yes, but I haven't done my finances for December yet," he claims but his nose twitches.

"Liar." I point to his nose.

"I haven't finished all of my finances for December yet," he amends.

"I don't care. Accept the money."

"I'm not taking your money."

I press the envelope against his chest and let go, but he doesn't catch it. He lets it fall to the floor as he walks away. "Told you. I won't take your money."

I pick the envelope up and chase after him. "I'm not a charity case."

He stops and glances over his shoulder at me. "No, you're not. You will pay me back."

I smile and hold out the envelope.

"Once the business is up and running."

"That's not our agreement."

He shrugs. "I don't care."

"Typical. You never care about my feelings."

He growls before stalking toward me. When he reaches me, he doesn't stop moving. I retreat until my back is up against the wall. He plants his hands on the wall and leans in. His wood and oil scent surrounds me and I inhale a deep breath. This is the scent I want coating my pillows.

"Your feelings are all I care about. All I think about."

Not true. If he cared, he'd open up to me. I glare up at him. "Don't lie to me."

He tucks a strand of hair behind my ear and I lock down my muscles before I lean into the warmth of his big, capable hand. "I thought you wanted me to lie to you."

"I don't want you to lie to me. I want you to tell me the truth." I place my hands on his chest and press. He doesn't budge.

He leans his forehead against mine. "I wish I could."

I notice my hands are caressing his chest and ball them into fists. "You can. You choose not to."

Pain flashes in his eyes before they fall closed. I decide to switch tactics and prove to him how stupid he's being.

"Unless you're working for some secret governmental organization and you had to leave on a mission to save the world. Riley Bragg, are you a super-secret spy?"

"I think spy infers secret."

"Or maybe you're a villain and you're on the FBI's most wanted list. You had to get out of town fast before the feds rolled in and put you away in some prison with no name in a secret place where you'd spend the rest of your life regretting your crimes."

"Darling, I'm too sexy to be a Bond villain."

Damn him. He's not wrong.

I tap my chin and pretend to consider the matter. "I can't come up with another plausible theory—"

"Those were supposed to be plausible theories?"

I ignore him. "Unless you're secretly married and your secret wife found out about us."

"I'm not fucking married."

My shoulders drop in relief. I know he's not married. But I was beginning to doubt myself because I seriously can't come up with a logical reason why a man would ghost me and then turn up three months later claiming he wants me back. It makes no sense!

"Good. Because if you're married, the inhabitants of Winter Falls will run you out of town. I've seen it happen before."

It's true. I have. The gossip gals want to buy pitchforks 'in case' they need to run another ruffian out of town. Their words. Not mine. Although I do enjoy the sound of ruffian.

He chuckles. "This town is crazy. I should have visited before."

Yeah, he should have. But I'm done with this conversation. If he doesn't want to tell me the truth, fine.

"Let's get back to work. We've got less than a month before Imbolc. And I will be open for the festival." I can't afford not to be.

He steps back and I duck under his arm to get some distance from him. One more second being trapped by his body and I would have jumped him. I mentally slap myself upside the head. *No, Moon. This man is not for you.*

"Can you grab a wrench out of your toolbox?" I ask, although I'd rather ask him to strip out of his flannel shirt. Flannel has never been this sexy before.

To his credit, he doesn't ask me what I need a wrench for. He's not entirely stupid.

"Yeah, sure."

He flips the lid of the toolbox open and reaches inside. But before he can touch the tool, he jerks his hand back and screams. "Snake!"

He tiptoes away from the box with his hands raised.

"Call the police! There's a snake in my toolbox."

"I don't think the police deal with animals."

"Then, call animal control."

"There's no animal control in Winter Falls."

He rushes to me. "We need to get out of here. It could be poisonous."

"I think you mean venomous."

He shackles my wrist as he tries to tug me out of the room. "Who cares about the proper vocabulary? We need to get out of here." I plant my feet. "Why aren't you running?"

"Why don't I have a look at the snake? Maybe it's a harmless garden snake."

"Are you crazy?" He shrieks. "No, don't answer."

"Riley Bragg, are you calling me crazy?"

"Now is not time for one of your arguments, Moon. We need to get out of here before the snake kills us both."

I roll my eyes. "Dramatic much?"

He freezes. "Why aren't you freaking out more?"

I shrug. "Maybe because I grew up here in a small town surrounded by nature."

He narrows his eyes on me. "Bullshit."

I widen my eyes. "Are you saying I'm a liar?"

"I'm saying you're up to something."

"I thought we needed to get out of here before we're killed by a ferocious animal?"

"Now I know you're up to no good."

I can't help it. Laughter bubbles up until it explodes from me. "You. Tiptoeing. Screaming." I manage to say between gasps for breath.

Riley crosses his arms over his chest. "Moon Star, are you pranking me?"

"Ding. Ding. Ding. You got the correct answer in one go."

He shakes his head. "I should have figured it out when you offered to check my toolbox. I know you hate snakes."

I do. It nearly killed me to put a rubber one in his toolbox but I'll go to great lengths to pull off the perfect prank. Witness me crawling into his basement window.

I wiggle my eyebrows. "Guess you don't know everything about me."

"I know a lot," he says before lunging for me. I try to get away but he tickles my ribs before I can escape.

"Stop," I yell between giggles.

He freezes. "What'll you do for me if I stop?"

"I won't tell your brothers what a sissy you are."

"No deal. You won't keep this incident to yourself."

He bends over to tickle my ribs again, but all I can see is his mouth approaching mine.

"Do not stare at my mouth like it's your last supper," he growls.

I bite my bottom lip. "I did skip breakfast."

"Fuck it," he mutters before his lips crash onto mine. He kisses me like he never wanted anything more. I certainly have never wanted anything more than his lips touching me, his hands exploring my body, his hard length pressing into me…

Bang! Bang! Bang!

"No hanky-panky on the diner floor," Feather shouts with a wag of her finger.

I wasn't about to… I notice my hands are on Riley's belt buckle. Crap. I was about to. I clear my throat.

"I have some administration work I should be doing," I lie and run away.

I refuse to think about how often I've run away from him recently. Moon Star doesn't run away from her problems. Unless the problem happens to be a six-foot-one-inch handyman with muscles for days. In such an event, running is not only allowed. It's encouraged.

Chapter 19

Bragg Brother Group Text

BRODY: RAISE YOUR HAND if you think Riley is the biggest idiot on the planet.

Miller: *emoji of man raising his hand*

Damon: *emoji of man raising his hand*

Elder: *gif of a llama raising his paw*

Riley: What the hell is going on? And why does Damon know?

Damon: I know everything.

Brody: Boo! Party foul!

Elder: *gif of llama throwing a yellow card*

Riley: What's with the llamas?

Brody: Avoidance. Classic move.

Brody added Peace to the conversation.

Peace: What's going on?

Brody: We're voting on Riley being the biggest idiot on the planet.

Peace: Don't you mean in the universe?

Riley: I'm not the one who insisted on being pants for Halloween.

Brody: Nothing wrong with being pants.

Riley: You were ten!

Brody: And I still got more candy than you.

Riley: Halloween is not a competition.

Brody: Says the loser.

Riley left the conversation.

Brody added Riley to the conversation.

Damon: Are we going to discuss why Riley's being an idiot?

Riley: No.

Brody: Ah, is someone pouting? Do you need your blankie?

Riley: I wasn't the one who carried a ratty security blanket around until I was five.

Brody: Do not dis Blake the blankie.

Damon: Some of us have lives. Can we skip the blame game and get to the reason why Riley's the biggest idiot in the universe?

Elder: Oh, some of us have big important lives. We can't relocate to Winter Falls because our job is too important.

Damon: Someone has to be there for Mom.

Elder: Which is why Mom called me to ask how you're enjoying Winter Falls since she hasn't heard from you.

Damon left the conversation.

Elder: Do we need to discuss what's going on with Damon now?

Miller: Can we finish this conversation sometime this year?

Elder: Someone's grumpy.

Damon re-joined the conversation.

Peace: Welcome back, Damon.

Miller: Peace is sucking up to Damon.

Elder: He's trying to keep the peace. Get it? Peace is keeping the peace.

Peace: Ha. Ha. I haven't heard that joke before.

Elder: You're welcome.

Damon: I'm only here because I'm concerned about Riley.

Riley: I'm fine.

Miller: No, he's not.

Elder: And we know Damon's here because he's afraid we're going to talk about him behind his back.

Damon: Maybe because you always do.

Brody: Maybe if you didn't eavesdrop all the time, you wouldn't know we talk about you behind your back all the time.

Riley: I don't talk about Damon behind his back all the time.

Peace: Suck up!

Riley: Dude, you don't know me.

Peace: But I can spot a suck up a mile away.

Riley: Is this part of your police training? Detecting when someone's sucking up.

Peace: No, but detecting when someone's lying is.

Brody: Which brings us around to today's topic – why is Riley lying to Moon?

Peace: You love her. You shouldn't lie to her.

Riley: Who said I love her?

Brody: Hold on. I rolled my eyes so hard my eyeballs got stuck in the back of my head.

Damon: You do know your eyeballs can't actually get stuck? Mom told you they could because she was tired of you rolling your eyes at her.

Peace: Speaking of moms. Mine asked if you want to come to Wednesday night dinner again.

Miller: Is Eagle cooking?

Peace: I'll take your answer as a yes.

Riley: I'm in.

Brody: In what? You certainly haven't been in Moon lately.

Peace: Wrong. They were practically having sex on the kitchen floor in the diner today.

Brody: Was this before or after he screamed like a little girl because of a rubber snake?

Riley: It looked real.

Brody: You're not denying you screamed like a little girl.

Riley: Don't make me sic Moon on you.

Damon: Finally! Let's discuss Moon.

Brody: Specifically, why is Riley being an idiot?

Riley: I'm not being an idiot.

Elder: Then why isn't Moon warming up your sheets right now?

Miller: What did you do wrong?

Riley: I didn't do anything wrong.

Brody: Snort.

Riley: What are you? A teenage girl? You don't write snort in a text message.

Brody: Snort. Snort.

Peace: I have it on good authority you refuse to tell her why you ghosted her.

Riley: Who's authority is this?

Peace: You can't keep a secret in this town.

Damon: Except the reason why our brother ghosted the woman he loves is still a secret.

Brody: I know why. And it's stupid. Beyond stupid.

Riley: You promised you wouldn't tell.

Brody: Does a promise count when you're being stupid?

Riley: Stop calling me stupid.

Brody: Stop being stupid!

Peace: Hate to break this up, but we don't use words like stupid in Winter Falls.

Brody: Stop being an idiot. You're not Dad.

Damon: Is this all because of Dad? I have to agree with Brody, you're being an idiot.

Riley: I don't want to be like Dad.

Miller: You're acting like Dad now.

Elder: Yep, you're being a dick and hurting the woman you love.

Brody: Total Dad move.

Damon: Fix this, Riley.

Riley: Fuck.

Peace: Should I be happy I never met my biological father?

Chapter 20

Make sure you don't hurl or you won't get the girl ~ Text from Elder to Riley

RILEY

I shove my hands in my pockets as I wait for Moon to answer her door. If she answers her door. She's not exactly talking to me. After our kiss yesterday, she hid the rest of the day in her office.

Her front door opens and there she is. My Moon. Today's the day I'm getting her back. But first.

"Can we talk?"

"What? No present?"

I considered buying her a gift, but I knew better. Moon cannot be bought. It was hard enough getting her to accept paying me a month late for my work at the diner.

"Moonbeam, I'll buy you all the presents in the world, but I know presents aren't what you want."

She plants her hands on her hips. "Really? What is it I want?"

I step close until my chest is nearly touching hers. I'm tempted to inch a bit closer. I want to feel her soft breasts against my hard chest. But now is not the time for horny Riley. I need to win Moon back first. Then, horny Riley can take the lead.

"You want someone who shows up. Someone who will never leave. Someone to watch horrible movies with you while you gab the entire time."

"Hey! My taste in movies isn't horrible."

I cock an eyebrow. "You watched *Skyscraper* five times."

"Have you seen Dwayne Johnson's arms?"

"*Suicide Squad.*"

"Kick-ass female protagonist."

"*Baywatch.*"

"Refer to my earlier Dwayne Johnson remark."

I could do this all day with her. She truly does have horrible taste in movies, but we've got more important things to discuss.

"May I come in?"

She frowns at me. Crap. Is she going to force me to confess my deepest, darkest secrets on her porch? But then her eyes narrow.

"Get in here," she ushers me inside before shouting across the street, "Don't think I don't see you, Sage!" and slamming the door.

"You seriously can't keep a secret in this town," I mutter.

"This is Winter Falls. If you can't handle it, leave."

She can't get rid of me that easily. I'm never leaving her again. "I'm not going anywhere."

She rolls her eyes. "Whatever."

I saunter to the living room and sit on her sofa.

"Make yourself at home, why don't you?"

I wink. "I am. Thanks."

"What do you want to talk about? Do you need the money after all? Let me go get it."

I shackle her wrist before she can walk away. "Why don't you sit down?" I pat the cushion next to me.

"Uh oh. This is a sitting down conversation? Do I need a drink first?"

She doesn't, but I may need one.

"Stop stalling."

She plops down in the corner of the sofa and crosses her arms over her chest. "You may begin."

"Thank you." I clear my throat. "I want to explain why I ghosted you."

Her eyes widen and her foot bounces. "You do?"

"Yep."

She twirls her hand in front of her. "You may proceed."

I chuckle. "Thanks."

"Um…" Maybe I should have let her stall because now that the time for me to confess has arrived, I have no idea where to begin. I should have come prepared. Made notes in advance.

"I freaked out when I discovered you were from Winter Falls."

Her brow wrinkles. "Okay."

"The week we were together. Best week of my life by the way."

"Stop brownnosing and get on with it."

It was worth a try. "The week we were together you told me tons of things about your hometown but you didn't say the name of the town until I was driving you to the airport."

"Forget a drink. I should prepare some food because this explanation is apparently going to take for-freaking-ever."

"Be patient. This is difficult for me."

She immediately sobers. "I'm sorry. Please continue."

"I knew the town of Winter Falls."

"Because your brothers, Miller and Elder, live here."

I nod. "And the reason they relocated here was to meet Peace, our half-brother."

Her forehead crinkles in confusion. I guess I have to connect the dots for her.

"Our half-brother who exists because our father cheated on our mother."

She snaps her fingers. "Oh right. Your parents were engaged when Clementine and your dad got together."

I don't question how she knows this. There really is no keeping a secret in Winter Falls.

"I'm sorry. It must have been difficult to learn you had a half-brother due to your father's infidelity."

She doesn't get it. "My father cheated on my mother all the time."

"All the time?"

"When I was a teenager, I caught him sneaking into the house in the middle of the night. He smelled of perfume and there was lipstick on his collar."

She grasps my hand and I hold onto her like the lifeline she is.

"I'm sorry, Riley. It couldn't have been easy finding out your father was unfaithful, but I'm confused as to what this revelation has to do with Winter Falls or me."

"I'm not explaining myself well."

She squeezes my hand. "Take your time. Use your words."

"The town of Winter Falls represents my dad's infidelity."

"Because proof of his infidelity is here. Live and in the flesh."

"I don't blame Peace," I'm quick to say. "It's not his fault."

"So you ghosted me because you didn't want to be in Winter Falls where Peace is? I said I'd move to San Diego to be with you."

"I didn't ghost you because you're from Winter Falls, but knowing you live here was a good reminder."

"A reminder of …"

"My genes." I swallow. "How I'm not a good man."

"I don't know what jeans have to do with this. You look mighty fine in yours." She waggles her eyebrows.

"Not my jeans. My g-e-n-e-s."

She rolls her eyes. "I know, but your comment was too stupid to dignify with an answer."

"Too stupid? You're calling me stupid?"

"Um, yeah. If you think being a cheater is a genetic trait, you need to go back to biology class."

"I passed biology class," I insist.

"You did? Because being a cheater isn't passed down. Eye color is inherited. Skin color is inherited. Blood group is inherited. Being a cheater isn't."

"But I grew up with him. He's the person who taught me how to be a man," I argue.

"And how did you feel about him cheating?"

I run a hand over my beard. "Horrible. My poor mom had no clue what he was doing. She loved him, doted on him, and he betrayed her."

"If you hate how his behavior affected other people, how could you possibly think you'd copy him?"

She's not getting it. "Growing up everyone said I was just like him."

"How were you like him?"

I don't want to discuss this, but I should have known she wouldn't be satisfied without insisting I lay my soul bare to her.

"We were both the starring pitchers of our high school baseball teams."

"And?"

"And what?"

"How else were you 'just like him'?"

"Isn't baseball enough?"

She snorts. "You're lucky being clueless is adorable on you."

I smirk. "You think I'm adorable."

She wags a finger at me. "Nuh-uh. No getting off track here. I'm going to set you straight once and for all."

I lower my voice. "Moonbeam, you can set me straight anytime you want."

"Being able to throw a baseball doesn't make you your father. You make the decisions as to how you want to act as a man.

Being upset your dad was a cheater is proof you're nothing like him. Do you understand?"

I'm still not convinced, but I don't admit this to Moon. I wouldn't put it past her to drag me to the high school for a lecture from the biology teacher. She doesn't get it. She doesn't understand how it feels to be compared to your father your entire childhood. Only to discover he's not the man you thought he was.

"Yes, I understand." It's not a complete lie. I do understand what she's saying. Believing her is a different matter.

She narrows her eyes on me. "I don't believe you."

"Do you want me to sign an affidavit? I can phone the family lawyer."

"Fine. I believe you."

I go in for the kill. "Does this mean you'll give me a second chance?"

"Hmm…I don't know."

She's wavering. I lift her up and set her on my lap.

"I love you, Moonbeam. Please give me – us – another chance. I don't want to live without you any longer."

She squirms in my lap. "I don't know. How can I trust you? What if some other secret comes to light? How do I know you won't go running?"

"I'm all out of secrets."

Her eyes narrow as she studies me. "You're sure? You're not going to discover you're the love child of John F. Kennedy and Marilyn Monroe and freak out on me?"

"Exactly how old do you think I am? They both died decades before I was born."

"Or maybe you're the secret baby of a hush hush governmental alien program. Have you ever been to Area 51?"

She smiles as she teases me, which means she's done fighting us. The weight on my shoulders lifts and I feel as if I can breathe for the first time in months.

I kiss her nose. "I'm not an alien."

"Are you certain?" She wiggles on my lap. "That's some tentacle you're hiding in your pants."

I lower my voice. "Maybe we need to explore this tentacle. Ensure it's not a harm to society."

"And how do you propose we perform this research?"

"I think I can come up with a few ideas," I whisper into her ear before I bite the lobe. She shivers in my arms.

She crawls out of my lap and offers me a hand. "At least this time farty dog won't be scoring your technique."

"I thought we agreed my technique deserved tens all around."

She barks out a laugh. "Not yet. But you can keep trying."

I throw her over my shoulder. "I am awfully good at practicing."

Chapter 21

I come to a halt on the sidewalk in front of the library. "This is a bad idea."

Riley frowns. "I thought you were done fighting us."

There's a difference between giving him a second chance and parading our relationship in front of the whole town. A town full of residents who think it's their right and privilege to stick their noses in our business.

"I am. I think the way I woke you up this morning proved it."

His eyes flare. "I want to wake up the same way every single morning for the rest of my life."

I roll my eyes. Typical man. "I'm not giving you a blow job every morning."

He wiggles his eyebrows. "Why not? I made it worth your while this morning."

Heat flashes through my body at the memory of his mouth on me. He totally made it worth my while.

"Get a room," Ashlyn calls as she joins us on the sidewalk. She's one to talk.

"You remember my best friend, Ashlyn."

Riley smirks before kissing her cheek. "It's lovely to see you again."

Rowan growls and pulls Ashlyn away from him.

"You must be Rowan."

Rowan grunts in response.

"He says it's nice to meet you, Riley." Rowan grunts again. "And you better treat our Moon right."

Rowan lifts his chin before grasping Ashlyn's hand and leading her into the library. We follow behind them.

"Does she interpret all of his grunts?" Riley asks.

"She claims she does, but she probably makes half of the stuff up. It is Ashlyn after all."

"No wonder you two are best friends," he grumbles and I pinch him.

We enter the library, which is set up for the Winter Falls monthly movie night, and run smack dab into the gossip gals. Riley immediately switches on the charm.

"Ladies, how lovely to see you." He actually does a little bow. "No pink sweatshirts today?"

"We couldn't agree on the saying." Sage glares at Feather.

"What are you glaring at me for?"

"Because you wanted a quote from that little green fellow."

"Yoda isn't a little green fellow."

"I still say we should have used *You sit on a throne of lies,*" Cayenne interrupts to say.

"No, no, no. *I'm gonna make him an offer he can't refuse* is the obvious choice," Clove says.

"You're all wrong. I already had the t-shirts with *Nobody puts baby in the corner* made," Petal says.

Ashlyn raises a fist in the air. "Nobody puts baby in the corner!"

Rowan grunts before tugging her away. She plants her feet and yanks on his hand. "Not in the corner! Nobody puts baby in the corner!"

Riley throws an arm around my shoulders. I can feel his body shaking with laughter. I elbow him.

"No making fun of the people of Winter Falls, handyman."

"Who's making fun? This is awesome."

I study his face for any signs of deception. His nose isn't twitching. Huh. He's telling the truth. Maybe small towns are growing on him.

"Yeah!" Juniper rushes toward us. "You made me ten bucks."

"You bet on whether we'd show tonight?"

"I had my doubts when you stalled on the sidewalk because you got scared."

"I wasn't scared." I wasn't. Not wanting to undergo an interrogation about your love life by the entire town is just plain smart.

She snorts. "Whatever."

"June Bug," Maverick cautions as he comes up behind his fiancé.

"What? I can spot a woman frightened of the gossip gals a mile away."

I ignore her comment since it's true and I have no intention of admitting to my fears anytime soon. "Maverick, have you met Riley yet?"

They barely have a chance to shake hands before Juniper is leading us away. "I have your loveseat reserved."

I groan. "You mean you have the hot seat reserved."

"This is too much fun. Moon Star going gaga over a man."

My brow wrinkles in confusion. "What do you mean? I've had boyfriends before. I'm not a hermit."

"Sorry. I merely meant you're always so independent. You can do everything all on your own. You don't need anybody."

She has no clue. I'm not all on my own by choice. I didn't ask my parents to abandon me. I did ask them to give me siblings. To no avail.

Riley wraps an arm around me. "You okay?"

"Why wouldn't I be?"

"Don't act flippant with me. I know you."

I sigh. "I'm fine."

He kisses my nose. "I know you're lying, but I understand you don't want to discuss this now in front of everyone."

"Discuss what?" Ashlyn asks around a mouthful of popcorn.

I groan. "Now do you understand why I hesitated on the sidewalk?"

The lights flicker and Juniper claps her hands to gain everyone's attention.

"Is everyone ready for movie night?"

"Ten bucks says the movie is *The Notebook*," Ashlyn shouts.

Rowan groans and she slaps him. "Hush you. It's a romantic second chance movie. It's perfect."

"Doesn't everyone know the movie in advance?" Riley asks.

"Nope. Juniper keeps it top secret."

"No way. A secret in Winter Falls?" He feigns clutching his chest.

I slap him. "Don't exaggerate. There are secrets in town."

He leans close to whisper in my ear. "Secrets like how you melt in my arms when I whisper in your ear."

He bites my earlobe and I shiver. Why did I insist we leave the house this evening? We could have been tearing up the sheets at this very moment.

"Ahem!" Juniper clears her throat and I jump in my seat.

"Busted," Elder shouts and I bury my face in Riley's chest.

"When did your brother arrive here?" I ask his shirt.

He glances behind him. "I think you mean brothers."

"Don't worry," Elder says. "You're not the first girl we've seen Riley making out with."

"Do you remember the time we busted him in the basement with the girl who got her hair caught in the zipper of his jeans?" Brody asks.

"You're not helping things," Riley yells at his brothers.

"Who said we're here to help?" Miller asks.

Juniper claps her hands again. "Tonight's movie is *The Ugly Truth*."

"No!" Sage shouts. "This is not allowed. You can't proceed to the next project before the current one is completed."

Juniper waves her arm toward us. "Mission complete."

Riley leans close to whisper in my ear. "What mission?"

"Project Do Over, remember?"

"They weren't joking?"

"The gossip gals do not joke about their matchmaking projects."

"The mission is not complete," Feather claims. "They haven't had their break up and dark night yet."

"Someone's been reading too many romance novels," Juniper mutters.

Feather gasps. "You can't read too many romance novels. It's impossible."

"It's also impossible our brother won't fuck things up with Moon," Brody says.

"I thought twins were super siblings who support each other," I say.

Riley frowns. "You obviously haven't met my twin."

Brody appears in front of us. "Brody Bragg at your service." I offer him my hand and he kisses my palm. "I'm the fun brother."

"You're a shit stirrer is what you are."

He winks. "Takes one to know one."

Riley kicks Brody's knee. "Get out of here."

Brody smirks. "Afraid I'm going to steal your girl?"

"She's way too smart for you."

"But, bro, she can cook." He rubs his stomach. "The machine needs to be fed."

"Enough." Riley stands.

"Oh, I'm scared." Brody scampers away.

"Sorry about him," Riley apologizes as he settles back down with me.

"He's funny," I tell him.

"You didn't grow up with him," he says. "Fuck. I'm sorry."

I shrug. "It's okay." And it is. I long ago accepted I'm a family of one.

Riley palms my neck and places his forehead against mine. "You're not alone anymore. You've got me and my family now."

I feign a cringe. "Maybe I don't want your nitwit brothers."

"I can't blame you there." He grins. "I guess we'll have to create our own family."

I narrow my eyes on him. "What do you mean?"

"Babies. As many as you want."

My heart hammers in my chest. Is he serious? He can't be serious. "We literally got back together yesterday and you're already discussing having children?"

"I know what I want. And I know what you want."

I cock an eyebrow. "And what is it you think I want?"

"A big family. A house full of laughter on Christmas day. A calendar on the refrigerator door full of ballet recitals, band rehearsals, baseball games, and school plays."

"H-h-how?" I clear my throat. "How can you possibly know that's what I want?" Because it is what I want. What I've always dreamed of.

"Moonbeam, I love you. I know you."

I swallow the lump in my throat. "But—"

He places a finger on my lip to stop me. "Don't answer now. Think about it. I'm ready to give you the world. Will you let me?"

I want to, but I'm afraid. What if he abandons me again? Can I trust him?

Chapter 22

"WHERE ARE WE GOING?" I ask Riley as we drive in his truck out of Winter Falls.

"It's a surprise."

I love surprises, but only when I figure out what the surprise is before it happens. I don't actually enjoy being startled. Huh. Maybe I don't love surprises after all.

"Can I guess? How many guesses do I get? Does it start with a P?"

He chuckles. "What starts with the letter P?"

"Playing pool, painting. Wait. Is it paintball? Say it's paintball." I raise my hands, fingers crossed in the air, and begin to chant, "Please be paintball. Please be paintball."

"You're in a dress and heels."

"What does my outfit have to do with anything? You're the one who told me to dress up."

"You're making my head spin."

I rub my hands together. "Good. My evil plan is working. Let the psychological warfare begin. I'm going to kick your ass in paintball."

He briefly glances over at me. "Really? Are you a secret paintball champion?"

"I've never done it before, but I'm sure I'll be awesome at it."

Racing around shooting your enemies? Sounds right up my alley. Although, I don't have any actual enemies. Unless you count Love Hill. She is not a nice person.

"Have you ever shot a rifle before?"

Ha! He thinks he knows everything about me. He doesn't! "Actually, I have."

He glances over at me with wide eyes. "Hold on. Hold on. Isn't Winter Falls all love and peace and no wars?"

"We're not all vegan tree huggers."

"I don't know. I could see Forest hugging trees all night long."

"He is a vegan, but I'm not. I do love a good piece of meat." I lick my lips.

He groans. "Don't say the word meat while licking your lips. You're making me hard."

I wag my finger at him. "Don't blame me. You get hard when there's a stiff breeze. Get it? Stiff."

He shakes his head. "You and Elder could be twins."

"Because we're both awesome. I like Elder. He was a good boss when I worked at the brewery. Miller, too, although he is the very definition of grumpy boss. Good thing I'm not into grumpy bosses or you wouldn't have a had a chance."

He growls. "Do you find Miller attractive?"

"Why? Are you jealous?"

"Answer the question."

Which means yes. He is jealous. This is going to be fun. "Miller's a good looking guy."

Riley snarls. "Did you go out with my brother?"

Uh oh. Snarly Riley is not fun. I place my hand on his thigh to calm him. "Ew. No. I'd kill him in his sleep. I'm teasing you. Miller's an attractive guy, but only because he resembles his brother, Riley, who is the most attractive of the Bragg bunch." I begin to sing, "The Bra-agg Bunch. The Bra-agg Bunch."

"There's one syllable in Bragg."

I smile at him. "Not anymore there isn't."

He places his hand over mine. "You're a nut job."

"I don't get the whole nut job thing. Nuts aren't a job. Nuts are delicious. Although what most people refer to as edible nuts are actually seeds or dry fruit."

He chuckles. "Thanks for proving you aren't a nut job."

I smile at him. "You're welcome."

He turns down a lane in the middle of nowhere. "This isn't the way to White Bridge."

"Who said we're going to White Bridge?"

Where else would we go? The city thirty minutes from Winter Falls is pretty much the only place within driving distance to enjoy a night out.

"Where are we going if…"

My voice trails off when a building comes into view. I gasp. I recognize it from *Architectural Digest*. The name, *The Mountain Lodge,* doesn't sound very elegant, but the place is beyond fancy. As in two Michelin stars level fancy. I've always wanted to eat here, but it's impossible to get a reservation.

And don't get me started on the cost. I'd have to sell a kidney to be able to afford this place.

"Holy macaroons! How did you get a reservation for this place?" I narrow my eyes on him. "Or did you make a reservation for a date with another woman ages ago and I'm substituting?"

"Don't be silly. You're my one and only."

I don't melt at those words. I don't. I'm being cautious this time with Riley. I am.

"The owners owed me a favor."

The owners of a Michelin-starred restaurant owed my handyman a favor? "What kind of favor?"

"I helped them out of a bind."

"A bind? As in whips and chains? Don't tell me you're a sadomasochist Dom on the side. Wait. Is that a thing? I have questions. Lots and lots of questions."

He chuckles. "I'm not a sadomasochist. And I'm not a Dom. I think you'd have figured out if I'm a Dom by now."

I snort. "As if you could ever control me."

"Moonbeam, don't lie. I know you get off on it when I take charge in the bedroom."

His voice comes out all gruff sounding and I wouldn't mind it if he took charge right here right now. But I'm not easy. Even if being easy ends up with me getting what I want. I like to make a man work for it.

"What favor did you do for the restaurant if it wasn't whipping the owner? Hold on. You said they were in a bind. Did you have to untie the owner after he was left all chained up in the basement?"

"You have quite the imagination."

"Thank you." I beam at him even though I know he wasn't trying to give me a compliment.

"They had a leak in the toilet before Christmas and couldn't find a plumber. I fixed it."

"Because you're Mr. Fix It."

"I prefer the term the world's best handyman."

I roll my eyes. "You would."

As soon as he parks his truck, I jump out and hurry toward the restaurant. Riley catches me before I can enter.

"Slow down, Moon. This isn't a military operation. There's no need to storm the restaurant."

Oops. I didn't realize I was running. "I'm a little excited."

"I'm glad."

He smiles and my body wonders why I haven't jumped him and dragged him into the woods to have my wicked way with him yet. He looks extremely jumpable this evening.

He's wearing khaki pants with a button down shirt. The sleeves are rolled up to his elbows showcasing his phenomenal forearms. And, yes, forearms can be phenomenal.

"You look handsome," I say before pushing up on my toes and kissing his jaw.

"And you're beautiful, Moonbeam."

His gaze focuses on my lips and I bite the bottom one. I can be a temptress when I want to. He moans and lowers his head toward me, but the door bangs open before we can touch.

"Later," he whispers.

"Promise?"

He winks before grasping my hand and leading me into the restaurant. My mouth drops open as I scan the inside. I wanted to come here for the food, but the interior of the place is amazing. It reminds me of a cabin lodge with its wooden floors and ceilings. And the view of the mountains out of the floor-length windows? Amazing.

"Mr. Bragg," the host greets us. "I have your table ready."

He leads us to a table for two in an alcove with its own private window.

"Are you sure you didn't whip someone for this table?" I ask once we're settled.

He laughs. I love the sound of his laughter. When we spent our week together on the beach in California, I loved to make him laugh.

"I have a joke."

"Let's hear it."

"A man walks into this fancy restaurant. When the waiter arrives, he asks: Can I have the sesame chicken, please? The waiter replies: I'm sorry, sir. This restaurant only serves French cuisine. He responds: Okay, can I …" I giggle. "Can I have some sesame chicken…" I giggle again. "S'il vous plait?"

Riley shakes his head. "You still can't tell a joke."

"I can, too." Our waiter arrives. "Do you want to hear a joke?"

His eyes widen. "Yes?"

"This guy has to go to a dinner at a fancy restaurant, but he forgot his tie so he used jumper cables. Do you know what the maître d' said to him?"

"Um, no?"

"I'll let ya in." I bark out a laugh. "But...d-d-on't start any-thing."

"Very amusing," he says before asking for our drink order.

I frown as he walks away. "He didn't think my joke was funny."

Riley reaches across the table to squeeze my hand. "Moon-beam, he couldn't understand your joke with all the laughing you were doing."

I shrug. "What can I say? I amuse myself."

"Mr. Bragg."

I glance up at the man who's standing next to our table and my eyes nearly bug out of my head. It's Mr. Fitzgerald, the owner of *The Mountain Lodge,* at our table. Holy cows have come home.

Riley stands and shakes his hand.

"I understand you're a chef," Mr. Fitzgerald greets me before I have a chance to figure out how to form words to speak.

"I-I-I am." I clear my throat and try the whole speaking thing again. "Yes, I am."

"Would you like a tour of our kitchen?"

"A tour of your kitchen?"

He smiles. "I thought you might." He offers me his elbow. "May I escort you?"

I spring out of my chair and lace my arm through his.

"You are so getting lucky for this later," I whisper to Riley as we pass him.

Caution is officially over with regard to Riley. I've loved him since the day we met. I loved him even when he ghosted me.

How can I not throw caution to the wind when he somehow manages to give me things I never thought I could have?

Maybe we should discuss having those children soon after all.

Chapter 23

What do you call a Peeping Tom with a hard on? A Popping Tom ~ Text from Elder to Riley

RILEY

I force myself to stick to the speed limit as I drive back to Winter Falls after dinner. Moon isn't making it easy for me. She's gliding her palm up and down my thigh. With every up glide, the tips of her fingers barely touch my cock before her hand retreats and glides down again.

I'm hard as a rock and ready to explode in my pants by the time I park the truck in front of my house. I shackle Moon's wrist and haul her into my lap before slamming my lips down on hers. Passion ignites the moment we touch. It always does.

She rocks in my lap as I thrust my tongue into her mouth. She tastes of cinnamon and sugar and I want to devour her whole. She kisses me like she's never wanted anything more. This isn't some means to an end. This is our slice of heaven.

Knock! Knock! Knock!

I wrench my lips from Moon's. "What the hell?"

An elderly man scowls at me. "If you're going to have sex, go inside."

Moon waves at him. "Hi, Mercury! Out for a late night walk?"

"Go inside, Moon."

"I thought you were done being a grumpy recluse."

I pinch her. "Don't call him a grumpy recluse."

She shrugs. "Why not? He is."

I roll down the window. "Mr. Mercury, I apologize."

He grunts. "It's Mercury. No mister involved. And she's not wrong."

Moon leans out of the window to kiss his cheek. "How are you?"

"I'm about to be tarred and feathered by those dang gossip gals who are watching you." He gestures toward the neighbor's house where the gossip gals are indeed standing on the porch scowling at the old man.

"Thanks for the warning."

He grunts in response before strolling away.

Moon opens the door and hops out of the truck. "Come on. Let's deal with that problem in your pants indoors."

"I wouldn't call it a problem," I mutter as I follow her to the front door.

The second I open the door, the dog attacks. He jumps up on Moon and she falls to her knees to pet him. He licks at her face while she gives him a rub down.

"Who's a good boy? Charlie's a good boy."

"You're supposed to be giving me a rub down," I complain.

"Shush. And go get Charlie Boy a treat. You deserve a treat, don't ya?"

I get a stick from the pantry and offer it to the dog. He ignores it. I can't blame him. I'd choose a rub down from Moon over a treat any day.

"Don't you want your treat? Aren't you feeling well?" Moon coos at him.

"Pretty sure he's feeling really good." I point to the proof of his excitement.

She squishes his face between her hands. "Charlie boy, I love you, but not in that way."

She pushes to her feet. "Should we get him a girl dog?"

"I'm not getting the visiting dog a girl dog to have sex with."

She raises her eyebrows. "You still believe Charlie is visiting?" She shakes her head. "You're silly, but we'll table the girl dog discussion for now."

I wrap an arm around her waist and draw her near. "Should we continue the activities we were enjoying before we were so rudely interrupted?"

She bats her eyelashes at me. "Activities? I think I need a reminder."

I thrust my hips and her eyes flare when she feels how hard I am. "How's this for a reminder?"

"I remember now," she breathes out.

Pfft.

How is it the fartiest dog in the world made his way into my life? I groan as I close my eyes and lay my forehead on Moon's. "What is it with all the interruptions today?"

She giggles before dancing away from me. "There's no dog in the bedroom." She rushes away and I hurry after her with the dog following me.

When I reach the bedroom, I use my foot to hold Charlie back. "No more interruptions," I say as I shut the door on him. He howls in response.

"We're ignoring him," I order Moon.

"Ignoring who?" she asks before whipping her dress off to reveal a matching red bra and panties.

I lay on the bed. "Come here."

She sticks out her bottom lip and pouts. "But you're fully dressed."

"I want you to sit on my face."

At my invitation, she doesn't waste any time diving for the bed and crawling up my body. As soon as I can reach her, I grab hold of her hips and position her until her covered pussy is poised over my mouth.

I tap her underwear. "These have got to go."

"I'm already way ahead of you." She pulls on the bows on the sides and the material falls open.

"Hell yeah," I murmur before spreading her lips open with my thumbs and licking her from core to clit.

She moans and I slap her ass. "Grab hold of the headboard."

She clutches onto the edge. "Oh, handyman, you say the nicest things."

I'm done talking. My cock is weeping, ready to dive into Moon, but she needs to come first. I want the taste of her on my tongue when I plunge into her.

I circle her clit with my tongue while I tease her opening with a finger.

"Stop torturing me," she urges as she widens her legs further until she's nearly suffocating me.

I flatten my tongue over her clit and sink two fingers into her at the same time. Her walls flutter around my fingers as I flick her clit with my tongue. I enjoy the feeling of her tightening around me as I pump my fingers into her over and over.

"Riley, Riley, Riley," she chants as she bounces on me.

Her excitement leaks from her and I remove my fingers to lap it up before spearing her with my tongue. She moans as she lifts her hands to toy with her nipples.

"I'm nearly…" She tumbles forward and her head hits the headboard with a loud clunk.

I stop and lift her so I can see her face. "Are you okay?"

"Do not stop."

I notice blood flowing from her nose down her face. "You're bleeding."

"And you're going to be bleeding if you stop."

"Are you serious? We need to check your wound."

"I am this close to coming. If you stop now, I'll cut your balls off and feed them to you in a meatloaf."

She wipes the back of her hand under her nose before grasping the headboard with her now bloody hands. "Fingers and mouth on me now."

I should probably refuse. She needs to be cleaned up, but she says the one thing guaranteed to make me do her will.

"Please, Riley. Please. Don't make me beg."

"Fine, but as soon as you come all over my tongue, we're cleaning your face."

"Sure. Whatever. Come all over your tongue first."

I use my hold on her hips to pull her down to my face and thrust my tongue into her. She bucks but I tighten my hold until I'm sure she'll have fingerprint bruises on her ass tomorrow. I don't care. She's not hitting her head again.

I growl and she clamps down on my tongue and moans, "Riley," as she climaxes.

I continue to plunge in and out of her until her inner walls stop spasming. As soon as she collapses, I pull her off of me and jackknife up. Her face is now covered in blood.

"Shit. We should have stopped."

She swats at me. "Don't ruin my Riley sex buzz."

"There's a Riley sex buzz?"

"Mmmhmm. But don't tell tomorrow Moon. Tomorrow Moon will deny its existence."

"Good to know you can be a nut when you're bleeding all over my sheets."

"Nuts are good," she sighs.

I roll off the bed and pick her up. "Time to clean you up."

I set her on the vanity in the attached bathroom. "Do you think it's broken?" I ask as I study her face.

She pats her nose. "Nope. Just a bloody nose."

"You're sure?"

"Yep. I know what a broken nose feels like."

I cock a brow. "You know what a broken nose feels like?"

"Some advice. Never play a sport with Ashlyn. Her husband may be the athlete in the family but she's the competitive one. She is the worst loser."

I kiss her forehead. "Okay, I'll take your word for it."

I wet a washcloth and begin cleaning the blood off of her face.

"I'm sorry I ruined our sexy times," she says when I'm rinsing out the washcloth.

I chuckle. "You didn't ruin anything, Moonbeam. You created a story we can tell to our grandchildren."

Her eyebrows raise. "You're going to tell our grandchildren stories about us having sex?"

"Nope. But I'm glad you admitted we will be having grandchildren."

She shrugs and glances away, but not before I notice the spark of excitement in her eyes. She can't fool me. She's ready to go all in with me.

Relief washes through me. Although she told me she'd give me a second chance, until this moment, I wasn't entirely convinced. I thought she was holding back. But now I know she's not. We're both all in.

Chapter 24

I'M SPREADING THE DOUGH on Riley's kitchen counter when he saunters into the room wearing a pair of pajama pants and nothing else. The thin material of his pajamas does nothing to hide his morning wood and I wonder why I crawled out of a warm bed with him in it.

He yawns and scratches his beard. "Why are you up already?"

Oh, right. There is a reason I left the bed. "I got this idea for a new recipe and I wanted to try it out."

He scans the counter where the dough for the cinnamon rolls is laid out. "Did I have all the ingredients you need?"

"Dude, have you seen your pantry? It's stocked better than the pantry at *Laduree*."

"What's Ladree?"

"Not Ladree. *Laduree*. It's a macaron shop in Paris. It's *the* macaron shop in Paris. They invented them."

His brow wrinkles. "When did you visit Paris?"

I slap him with a towel. "You know I've never been. But I imagine the pantry at *Laduree* isn't as well stocked as yours is."

I'm not exaggerating. It's ridiculous how full his pantry is. Especially considering how large the room is to begin with. My spare bedroom is smaller.

"What were you planning to do? Invite the entire town over for a meal?"

He shrugs. "I wanted to make sure you have everything you need in case…"

I raise my eyebrows. "In case of what?"

I know exactly what he means, but sometimes a woman enjoys hearing a man wants her. He wraps an arm around my waist and draws me near.

I bat him away. "I'm covered in flour."

"And I don't give the first fuck." He trails his nose along mine. "I filled my pantry full of everything I could think of that you could possibly need to cook and bake in my kitchen in case you ever granted me a second chance."

I practically melt in his arms, but I'm not letting him off the hook just yet.

"You expect me to cook and bake for you every day?"

"I remember," he rumbles and my breath gets caught in my throat. "I remember how you cooked for me every morning, how excited you got when you thought up a new recipe, how pushy you were when you wanted me to sample one of your inventions. I haven't forgotten a thing about our week together."

"I'm not pushy," I claim because sometimes stubborn wins out over my body's wants.

He chuckles. "And you're not the woman who insisted I continue to eat her out despite blood pouring down her face."

I slap his chest. "I was close."

Heat flares in his eyes. "Yeah, you were. You exploded on my tongue not thirty seconds later."

My core warms at the reminder. "I don't remember," I lie.

"You need a reminder?" He punches his hips and his hard length hits my stomach causing sparks to explode throughout my body.

"Yes," I breathe out as I push up on my toes to reach his mouth.

I bite his bottom lip and he moans before molding his lips to mine. I sigh and he uses the opportunity to slip his tongue into my mouth. My tongue meets his and we duel for supremacy until he growls and his hand fists my hair to tilt my head to his liking.

Beep. Beep. Beep.

At the blare of the oven timer, I jerk away from him. "The biscuits."

I rush to the oven and yank the door open. I'm reaching inside to remove the tray when Riley elbows me out of the way.

"Your hands are not fireproof," he admonishes as he removes the biscuits from the oven and sets them on the counter.

I perch my hands on my hips. "It's your fault for distracting me."

"If accepting the blame means I have the taste of you on my tongue, I'm in." He winks.

I use my hip to push him out of the way. "Go. Sit down. Breakfast is almost ready."

He frowns at the dough on the counter. "This doesn't appear anywhere near ready."

"Those are for later." I lift the lid from the pan on the stove. "This is for breakfast."

He leans close to sniff the contents. His stomach rumbles. "I'll set the table."

He's already sitting at the table waiting by the time I arrive with plates of biscuits and gravy.

"You're drooling," I tease.

"I don't care. It's been three months since you've cooked for me."

"And who's fault is that?"

He freezes with a forkful of food inches from his mouth. He clears his throat before laying the fork down.

"Is this how it's going to be?"

I open my mouth to deny it, but I don't want to lie. I'm done with all the lies and misunderstandings between us.

"I don't know."

"If we're going to make a go of us, you can't bring up my mistake every time you're mad at me."

I nod. My head knows this. My heart? Not so much. It wants him to suffer as much as I did for the three months we were apart.

"I did suffer," he says proving he can read my mind. I scowl at him. "What? I know you. I know what you're thinking."

"No, you don't."

"You're thinking you want me to suffer as much as you did. You're thinking I didn't suffer for those three months. You're thinking is jacked."

"Hey! It's not okay to make fun of someone's thinking."

"I'm not making fun. I'm trying to show you how wrong you are."

"Saying you suffered doesn't prove anything."

He stands before pointing at me. "Stay there."

I'm not going anywhere. Not when he has my curiosity piqued. Curiosity may have killed the cat, but it's never hurt me before.

"Here." He slams a picture frame down on the table. I gasp. It's a picture of us on the beach.

"This picture has been on my nightstand every single night for the past three months."

"But it wasn't there last night." I think I would have noticed a picture of us together in his bedroom.

"I put it in the drawer. I thought you might freak out if you saw it."

I bite my lip as my finger traces his face on the picture. There's nothing to say. I totally would have freaked out if I saw the picture there the first time we had sex.

"And this." He drops his wallet on top of the picture frame.

"What's your wallet got to do with anything?"

"Open it up."

I should probably be the type of person who hesitates at this point. But I'm not. And I don't. I'm curious. Besides, he offered. I open the wallet to discover a picture of me staring back at me.

"I remember when you took this picture."

He chuckles. "You were mad."

"Duh. I had sex hair and my lips were swollen."

"Sexiest woman I've ever seen."

I hand the wallet back to him.

"Do you understand now how I suffered? I had met the woman of my dreams, but I couldn't have her."

I snort. "Because you flunked out of biology class."

He brushes the hair off of my neck and kisses me there. "I'm done denying myself the woman I want. I'm all in. Can you get over what I did to you?"

I blow out a breath. I want everything with Riley. A wedding ring, kids, the whole shebang. But it's hard to forget how he abandoned me. If I want everything, though, I'm going to have to figure it out. "I'm trying."

"Good. We're moving forward. In fact, you're coming with me to the Wednesday night Bragg slash Sky family shit show."

I giggle. "Shit show? You know I love a good shit show."

He draws a hand over my cheek before moving to sit across from me. "Great because I'm hungry and it's a sin to let any food you've made get cold or go to waste."

He digs into his biscuits and gravy and doesn't stop until his fork clatters to the table.

"I'm surprised you're not licking your plate."

"I considered it, but I can't eat one more thing or I'll explode." He rubs his stomach.

I roll my eyes. "No one forced you to eat six biscuits."

"I'm going to gain fifty pounds if you cook for me every morning."

A tendril of excitement bolts through me at the idea of cooking for him every morning. I want to wake up with him every day after a night of getting all sweaty in the sheets. Of course, I do. I love him. I don't want to ever be apart from him again. But saying those words after what happened isn't easy.

I know. I know. I said I'd tried to forget what happened but it hasn't been an hour since I made my promise. I'm allowed some time to figure things out.

I force those thoughts out of my mind. "I guess you'll have to come up with some inventive ways to burn those calories off." I waggle my eyebrows

His nostrils flare as he pushes to his feet. "How long does the dough need to rise?"

I don't know what's sexier. Riley in a hurry to drag me back to the bedroom or him knowing dough needs to rise.

"Two hours."

He pulls my chair out before offering me his hand. "Plenty of time to burn off some of those calories."

I take his hand and he hauls me to my feet before hurrying toward the stairs while dragging me behind him.

"In a hurry?"

"We have a lot of wasted time to make up for."

I giggle as I rush to keep up with him. I'm one hundred percent on board with his plan to make up for lost time.

Chapter 25

"I CAN'T BELIEVE YOU made cinnamon rolls for the entire town," Riley says as we climb the stairs to the courthouse for the monthly business meeting.

My first one as mayor. A position I didn't ask for and definitely don't want. What do I know about being mayor? I can barely manage the renovations of the diner. How am I supposed to manage the business of the entire town?

I shove the fear away and grin at Riley. "You're only whining because you planned to eat all of them."

"Duh. I'm only with you because of your skills in the kitchen."

I stop. "Really? You didn't enjoy my skills with my mouth this morning?"

He smirks. "I guess your skills in the bedroom aren't bad either."

"You guess? Well, then, I guess I won't be telling you where the extra tray of cinnamon rolls I made for you is," I say and walk away.

He rushes after me. "You made an extra tray for me?"

Elder opens the door. "This is priceless. My little brother is literally chasing after you."

I wiggle my eyebrows. "I can't help it I'm irresistible."

He chuckles. "I've missed you at *Naked Falls Brewing.*"

"I am pretty irreplaceable."

Miller comes up behind Elder. "If by irreplaceable you mean someone who yells at customers, then yes, you are irreplaceable."

"I've told you a million times it wasn't my fault. She was the one who ordered a slice of chocolate cake with beer. I will not abide by someone drinking beer while eating my cake."

"Can you two stop flirting with my woman and help me carry these trays into the meeting?" Riley grumbles from behind me.

Elder's eyes widen. "Did you make your cinnamon rolls?"

"It's a new recipe."

"Tastes good," Miller mumbles around a mouthful of roll.

"This is not how you help," Riley complains.

Miller shrugs. "One less roll to carry. You're welcome."

"Moon brought cinnamon rolls!" Ashlyn shouts as she rushes toward us. "Give me five."

I hand her a roll. "You'll get one and be happy."

"Give me four more and I'll give you Rowan's red velvet pancake recipe."

I snort. "You can't bargain with something you don't have."

"All you have to do is break into our safe and the recipe's yours."

Her hand reaches out for another roll and I slap it. "No! I'm not breaking into a safe for a recipe I don't need."

"Ow. Now I'm hurt and you have to give me another roll or I'll sue you." She bats her eyelashes at me.

"You can't manipulate me."

She snorts. "Did you forget about the time I convinced you to prank Riley?"

"Did you forget about the time I broke your hand?"

Her nose wrinkles in confusion. "You never broke my hand."

"Yet. I haven't broken your hand yet."

"You're mean." She stomps away. "Rowan, Moon's being mean to me!"

Riley nudges me. "Where do you want these trays?"

"Next to the beer and popcorn."

I barely make it two steps into the room before Lilac approaches me. "We need to discuss a few things before the meeting begins."

Miller swoops in. "I'll take those cinnamon rolls off of your hands."

"Don't eat them all," I call after him.

"I make no promises."

Lilac frowns at me. "Why did you bring cinnamon rolls to the meeting?"

I shrug. "I'm trying out a new recipe."

I am, but it's not the reason I spent all night baking.

She cocks her head as she studies me.

"What did you need to discuss?" I ask before she can speak.

Everyone assumes Lilac isn't perceptive because she doesn't understand social cues. Everyone's wrong. She's entirely too insightful when you're the new mayor trying to buy everyone off with cinnamon rolls.

She clears her voice. "The annual budget for town festivities, preparation for Imbolc, and the expansion of the brewery."

"Expansion?"

At her nod, I search the room for Eden. I hope she's not here. She is not going to be happy when she finds out the brewery expansion is a go. She spent the better part of last year while she was mayor thwarting Miller and Elder's application to expand *Naked Falls Brewing*.

I spot her standing with Harmony and Soleil and wave. She smiles at me and gives me a thumbs-up. She won't be smiling at me once she learns about the brewery expansion. This being mayor thing is going to be trickier than I expected and I already expected it to be tricky.

Lilac taps her watch. "Time to begin."

Nothing happens on time in Winter Falls unless Lilac's involved. I swear she was born with a watch strapped to her wrist.

I take my place behind the table in the front of the room and Ashlyn rushes to me. She slams a beer down on the table.

"The word of the day is I," she declares before fleeing.

"I'm not participating in a drinking game while I'm the mayor," I shout after her.

"Drink!" is her response.

"Ignore her," Lilac says.

"You love me and you know it!"

Lilac shakes her head at Ashlyn's outburst. "Because Mom insists I love my siblings."

"And their spouses," her mom chimes in.

I giggle at their antics. The West family is fun and crazy and I wish they were my family. But no, I'm stuck with Mr. and Mrs. Being Tied Down Is Torture. My stomach burns at the reminder of my parents.

Riley catches my eye and mouths, *Good luck, Ms. Mayor.*

The burn of betrayal is replaced by tingles of excitement. Riley winks and I wish we could skip this meeting, but Lilac elbows me. "Time to start."

"The January business meeting of Winter Falls is hereby called to order."

"Boo!" Ashlyn hisses. "She avoided the use of the word I, but now I said it. Drink twice, suckers!"

I ignore her. "Lilac has the floor."

Several people groan as Lilac stands next to me. If I weren't sitting in front of everyone, I'd be groaning, too. Don't get me wrong. I like Ashlyn's sister, but when she begins with figures and budgets, it's snoozeville for me.

"Ahem."

I startle and glance up at her. I guess it's snoozeville when Lilac discusses numbers no matter whether I'm mayor or not. "What?"

"It's time for the next agenda point." She taps the agenda item with her pen.

Crap. This is going to be bad. "Do I have to?" I whine.

"Rip off the bandage."

I blow out a puff of air and stand. "The expansion of *Naked Falls Brewing*," I catch Eden's gaze and notice she's already scowling, "has been approved."

"This is bullshit!" she shouts.

Miller growls. "You not getting your way doesn't mean it's bullshit."

"Yes, it is! Your expansion will affect my garden. I thought Winter Falls was all about sustainability and local produce. I call bullshit."

Miller glares at her. "Selfish."

Mercury taps his cane on the floor a few times. "Eden's right. The brewery doesn't need to expand. It's fine the way it is."

"An old-timer being afraid of change is not a reason to deny our expansion," Miller grumbles.

"You better do something about this Moon." Eden points at me and several other people stand and join her protest.

"Plants before beer!" someone shouts and soon everyone is shouting.

"Enough!" Riley booms as he pushes to his feet and quiet descends on the room. "You will stop giving Moon a hard time about this or you'll deal with me."

Feather fans her face. "I do love a good alpha."

She's not alone. I'm practically melting in my seat after Riley's declaration.

Petal nods her approval. "I knew we matched the right man with Moon."

I wag my finger at the group of troublemakers. "You didn't match Riley with me. We were together before you even met him."

"But you weren't together when he moved to Winter Falls, which is where we came in," Sage points out.

I cross my arms over my chest. "You didn't do anything besides make bets and spy on us."

"What about you needing a new handyman because my husband suddenly wanted to retire to go on yoga retreats with me?" Clove asks with a wink.

I groan. I should have known the gossip gals were behind Sirius' abrupt retirement.

"And have you forgotten about karaoke? I have it on good authority the night ended spectacularly for you." Cayenne wiggles her eyebrows in case I forgot how spectacularly the night ended for me. No worry there. I didn't forget. Because it was pretty spectacular.

"Project Do Over is my favorite," Petal declares.

Sage grunts. "You say every project is your favorite until the next one comes along."

Petal purses her lips. "I don't think the next project is going to turn out well."

"I told you." Feather huffs. "It's not time for the next project yet."

Sage nods. "She's right. Project Do Over isn't complete."

I bang the gavel down on the table. "Enough! This is a business meeting."

"Which is why we're discussing the business of you and Riley," Sage says.

I bang the gavel again. "No! My relationship is not up for discussion."

Ashlyn raises her hand. "Is your theft of my gavel up for discussion?"

I roll my eyes. "It's not your gavel."

"You stole it from my house."

"Having the gavel in your home doesn't make it your property." Although, she's right. I did steal it from her house. It's not my fault she didn't lock it up.

"Possession is nine-tenths of the law."

I wave the gavel in the air. "In which case, this gavel is now mine as it's in my possession."

She jumps to her feet and rushes toward me, but Rowan catches her before she can make it two feet. "Enough, dream girl."

I take advantage of Ashlyn being under control. "Meeting dismissed."

Riley appears at my side. "Do you need me to escort you out of here?"

"Why? Are you afraid the people of Winter Falls are going to mob me?" I pat his chest. "They're more likely to stage a sit-in." A picture of him wearing sunglasses while crossing his arms over his chest and guarding me flits through my mind. "Although, we can play bodyguard."

"We can? Do I get to guard every single inch of you?" he whispers into my ear and I shiver.

"Who said you're the bodyguard?" Told you I'm not easy.

He lowers his voice, "Moonbeam, I am the bodyguard."

Warmth flows through me to my core. I'm one hundred percent on board with this fantasy.

Chapter 26

I stop on the sidewalk in front of Peace's parents' house. "Maybe this isn't a good idea."

I don't know if I'm ready to join Riley for a family dinner. I haven't been to a family dinner in forever. When my parents first left, I joined Ashlyn's family every once in a while for a Sunday meal but then she went off to college and I was left on my own again.

Riley frowns at me. "Why not? I thought we agreed we're serious."

I chew on my bottom lip. "We did but…"

He palms my neck and hauls me near. "There's no reason to be afraid."

I bristle. No one calls Moon Star a scaredy-cat. I am not afraid of anything. I will take the world on all by myself if necessary.

"I am not afraid."

He leans his forehead against mine. "I'm not leaving you again. I promise. I love you."

I let his words wash over me before inhaling a deep breath and nodding. "Okay. I'm ready."

"Ready for what?" Brody asks as he joins us. "The horizontal mamba?" He thrusts his hips.

"What if I prefer to be on top?" I ask with a waggle of my eyebrows.

Riley groans. "No, don't engage him. You'll encourage him."

I grin up at him. "Maybe I enjoy encouraging him."

He kisses my nose. "You're a troublemaker."

He grasps my hand and leads me toward the house. The door opens before we reach the porch.

"I was wondering how long you needed to stand out there to convince Moon to join us," Peace says.

Elder pops up behind him. "What do a penis and a Rubik's Cube have in common?"

Peace elbows him. "No dirty jokes in my mom's house."

Elder wiggles his eyebrows. "Who says it's dirty?"

"Is your name Elder?" I tease. Because if it's Elder, it's dirty. The man never met a joke he couldn't dirty up.

He winks at me. "I'll tell you later."

Riley growls at him. "Don't tell my girlfriend dirty jokes."

"It's Moon. She tells dirty jokes all the time."

"Is everyone going to stand in the doorway or are you coming inside?" Mrs. Sky asks.

Miller shoves past us to enter. "It smells delicious in here."

Elder shakes his head. "My twin will eat you out of house and home if you let him."

"Hi, Mrs. Sky." I offer her the cake I made. "I hope you like chocolate."

"Did you bring me your death by chocolate cake?" she asks and I nod.

Brody slaps Riley on the back. "You're going to get fat married to this one."

Married? We've been back together for a minute. I'm not ready to talk wedding bells. Although, I shouldn't be surprised. We've already discussed kids.

Riley wraps an arm around me. "Don't worry. We've already figured out a way for me to burn off the calories."

I elbow him. "If you discuss our sex lives with your brothers, I'm telling them how you gave me a bloody nose."

Brody rubs his hands together. "This is better than I could have ever imagined. Tell us more about this bloody nose."

"I had a nosebleed in the shower. It was a blood bath." Elder chuckles and holds up his hand. I high-five him.

Eagle strolls into the hallway from the kitchen.

I nod at him. "Eagle."

"Moon."

"Can you say awkward?" Elder sings.

"Why? What's wrong?" Riley frowns down at me. "Is this why you didn't want to come? Do I need to kick his ass?"

"What is it with you and kicking people's asses? Violence is not allowed in Winter Falls."

"I don't think violence is allowed anywhere," Brody points out. "It's why there are laws against it."

Peace shoves him. "Smart ass. You knew what she meant."

The door bangs open and Olivia rushes in. "Sorry. My yoga class ran late. What did I miss?"

"Moon and Eagle are doing this weird stare down, but I have no idea what's happening," Brody answers.

"I know!" Elder raises his hand and jumps up and down.

Clementine frowns at him. "No jumping in the house."

Elder freezes. "Sorry, Mrs. Sky."

"Should I leave?" I ask when Eagle continues to stare at me. "I'm sorry, Mrs. Sky. I didn't intend to interrupt your family gathering."

"Stop," she orders when I turn to leave. "One, my name is Clementine. Two, you aren't leaving." She glares at Eagle. "You aren't the one who should apologize."

"I'm sorry, Moon," Eagle immediately says.

"What's he sorry for?" Olivia asks.

"He took a job cooking for us at the brewery and left Moon high and dry," Miller explains.

"I don't blame you," I say to Eagle. "I couldn't pay you during the months the diner was closed due to the renovations. I understand you need to provide for your family."

"But what are you going to do when you open?" Eagle asks.

"I'll figure it out." The same way I always figure everything out.

"You can't cook seven days a week and manage the business," he says.

"I plan to close one day a week and we won't be open for dinner. At least, not at the beginning."

"It's still a lot."

I know, but what choice do I have? It's not as if cooks are dying to live in the small town of Winter Falls. I'll find one, though. Eventually.

"You should quit the brewery," Clementine tells her husband.

"Whoa! Hold up." Elder raises his palms. "We need a cook as much as the diner does."

She dismisses his concern with a flick of her hand. "You'll find someone else. Moon needs Eagle more."

"We need Eagle," Miller grumbles.

Brody claps his hands. "This is awesome."

I bury my face in my hands. This is not awesome. I'm causing a rift between Riley and his new extended family.

"No!" Clementine insists. "Eagle will quit the brewery and work at the diner. When will you re-open?"

This can't be happening. I must be dreaming.

"Why are you being nice to me?"

I'm not begging for compliments or asking for pretty words. I'm seriously confused. I know Clementine. It's a small town. I know everyone. But we're not close. And she's never stood up for me before.

She grasps my hands. "Because I should have stepped forward when your parents left. But I didn't. I did exactly what everyone in this town did. I left you on your own."

"I was fine."

She squeezes my hands. "You survived on your own, but you could have thrived if Atlas and Azalea hadn't left you alone."

I square my shoulders. "I did thrive. I'm twenty-five and a business owner. Maybe the business isn't open yet, but it will be soon."

I don't need anyone to help me with anything. I can do it all on my own.

"I'm not saying you can't do everything. I'm saying you should have had people cheering you on from the sidelines. Well, guess what? I just appointed myself head cheerleader."

Olivia raises her hand. "I'm in!"

"I had people. Ashlyn and her family," I argue because Clementine's making me sound pathetic. I'm not pathetic.

"I told Ruby she should have let you live with her family, but she was too busy dealing with Ashlyn and her four sisters. She didn't have room for you. I should have stood up. You should have lived here."

"Mom." Peace wraps an arm around her shoulders. "You can't blame yourself."

"Who should I blame then? Huh? I let a sixteen-year-old girl live on her own because I was too timid to speak out. No more. You hear me, Moon. No more. I don't care what happens with Riley."

"Hey!" Riley interrupts.

"I'm here for you whether you're with Riley or not," she clarifies.

Riley growls. "She'll be with me."

"I don't know how to respond," I tell Clementine.

And I don't. I never resented the older generation for letting my parents leave me all alone. *Yes, you did,* a voice in my mind,

I usually ignore, whispers. Fine. I did resent them. This whole town sticks up for each other and yet no one stuck up for me.

"No one's ever gone to bat for me before," I whisper but Clementine hears me.

"Everyone assumed you'd reach out if you needed anything," she says.

Olivia snorts. "Have they never been around teenagers before?"

Clementine ignores her to continue, "And you didn't have any problems. Unless you count getting in trouble with Ashlyn, which you know the people of Winter Falls don't."

I sniff to stop the tears welling in my eyes from falling. I can't believe this is happening. I always wanted someone to adopt me after my parents left. Sometimes before my parents left, too. Their belief in 'no boundaries' didn't exactly lead to a nurturing environment for a little girl.

Riley wraps his arms around me. "Don't cry, Moonbeam." He rocks me back and forth. "We'll figure this out. We'll find you a cook. But don't cry. I can't handle your tears."

"I'm not crying. My eyes are watering because of Elder's perfume," I claim.

Elder doesn't miss a beat. "What can I say? The ladies think I smell delicious."

Riley smacks him upside the head. "Knock it off."

"Are we done with the heart-to-hearts now?" Miller asks and Riley snaps his teeth at him. "What? Can you not smell the scent of meatloaf wafting from the kitchen. Eagle makes the best meatloaf."

I push away from Riley. "Hold on. Are you saying Eagle's meatloaf is better than mine?"

"I've never tasted yours," Miller claims.

I point to him. "Saturday. My house. Come hungry."

He rubs his belly. "I'm always hungry."

"Let's sit before the food gets cold." Clementine ushers everyone into the dining room.

Peace holds out a chair for Olivia before pulling the seat next to her out and sitting down.

Pffffffft.

Brody bursts into laughter. "You farted."

Peace picks the whoopee cushion off of the chair and rushes after Brody who dashes outside yelling, "It's not my fault you have gas."

"What do you think?" Riley asks while everyone's distracted by Brody's antics. "You ready to be a part of this family?"

"It depends."

He tucks a strand of hair behind my ear. "On what? Anything you want, it's yours."

"If everyone can agree my meatloaf is the best."

He buries his face in my shoulder as he bursts into laughter. I glance around the table. Miller and Elder are fighting over whose slice of meatloaf is bigger. Olivia is cheering for Peace to kick Brody's ass. Clementine and Eagle have their heads together and are speaking in hushed tones.

This is what I've been missing. This is what I've always wanted. How can I not love Riley when he gives me everything I've ever wanted?

Chapter 27

RILEY

"I'm not swimming in that freezing cold river again," I say when I open my door to Brody.

"Are you afraid your tiny little balls will shrink to the size of marbles?"

Hell yeah, I am. It took days before my balls recovered from our last swim. He can't tell me his balls faired any better, but I'm not discussing my balls with my brother. Some lines are not meant to be crossed even if we did share a womb for nine months.

I shove him out of the doorway and shut the door behind me. Charlie howls in response to being left alone.

"You still have the dog?"

"His name is Charlie."

Brody chuckles. "I thought you hated animals."

How can I hate Charlie? Yes, he's farty and stinks up the house. And, okay, it's creepy how he stares at Moon and me while we're having sex. But he's also a good companion. Besides, Moon loves him. I'm never getting rid of him.

"Whatever." I shrug. "What is this big, important meeting about?"

"Miller and Elder said they have something 'important' to discuss. I don't know what."

We arrive at *Naked Falls Brewing* where Miller and Elder have demanded our presence this morning within a few minutes. I'd rather be in bed with Moon, but she's at the diner working even though it's Sunday morning.

When we enter the brewery through the back door, it's not Miller and Elder waiting for us, it's Damon.

I hug him in greeting. "I didn't know you were in town."

"Just got in."

"Did you change your mind about moving to Winter Falls?"

"No. I was summoned." He frowns. "Since when do Elder and Miller summon us?"

Brody elbows him. "Being the oldest brother doesn't mean you're in charge of us."

Damon cocks an eyebrow. "It doesn't? Then, who got you out of trouble at school when the teacher found you putting a dead rabbit in Bill's locker?"

"It wasn't my fault."

"A dead rabbit magically appeared in your arms as you were breaking into his locker?"

"Bill was asking for it."

I grunt. "Bill was asking for it? Aren't you the one who put itching powder in his jockstrap?"

Brody crosses his arms over his chest and glares at me. "Because he stole my girl."

I snort. "He didn't steal Melissa. She broke up with you after you pantsed her in front of the entire school at the pep rally."

"Everybody laughed."

"At her. Everybody laughed at her. She was humiliated." I point out.

"I don't know why. I did it to Robin and she thought it was hilarious."

"Robin wasn't your girlfriend. She was your best friend."

He shrugs. "She was a girl."

Elder and Miller join us. "What are we discussing?" Elder asks.

Brody puffs out his chest. "How awesome I am and how old Damon is."

"Damon is pretty old," Elder says.

Damon scowls. "I'm one year older than you and Miller."

Elder shakes his head. "Getting forgetful in his old age. It's two years."

Peace rushes in through the back door. "What's going on? Sage said you called in a disturbance. I hope you aren't fighting with Eden again. You know you're on the gossip gals' radar."

Brody rubs his hands together. "This is awesome. I can't wait to watch how this plays out."

Miller growls. "Nothing is playing out."

"Hold on," Damon says. "Who are the gossip gals and what are you talking about?"

"Sorry." Brody feigns zipping his lips. "Need to know information limited to Winter Falls residents."

Damon crosses his arms over his chest and scowls at Brody. "Who are the gossip gals?"

Brody hides behind me. "Take him. He's the older brother."

I shove him so he can't hide behind me anymore. "For someone who thinks a good prank is causing a person to shit his pants, you're quite the pansy."

"He wasn't supposed to shit his pants. He was only supposed to get gas. Really loud gas."

Peace purses his lips. "Do I need to keep an eye out for Brody's enemies?"

"I don't have any enemies in Winter Falls."

"Yet," Elder, Miller, Damon, and I say in unison.

Peace shakes his head. "If there's no emergency, I better get back to patrol."

"Wait," Elder says. "We have an announcement."

"Let me guess." Brody bounces on his toes. "You're shaving off all of your hair and joining a convent."

Elder rolls his eyes. "Idiot. Women join convents. Men join monasteries."

"I'm not shaving off my hair," Miller grumbles.

"I want another guess." Brody bites his lip as he considers. "You're selling the brewery to join a nudist colony in Antarctica."

"No one lives in Antarctica," I say.

Elder shivers. "Who would want to be naked in Antarctica?"

"Good point." Brody nods. "How about—"

"No." Elder cuts him off with a swipe of his hand. "You're never going to guess this anyway."

"Although, it's not a surprise," Miller adds.

"You know how we found Peace," Elder begins.

"He's not the only one," Miller says.

"Hold up. We have more half-brothers out there?" I can't fucking believe this. Dad was such an asshole.

Elder shrugs. "We may have. This match isn't as conclusive as the previous ones."

I blow out a breath of air. "Dad never could keep it in his pants."

Peace's brow wrinkles. "Wait. I thought he only cheated on your mom when they were engaged."

I snort. "Not likely. I caught him coming home smelling of perfume and wearing lipstick."

Brody raises his hand. "Me too."

Elder nods. "Me three."

Miller grunts. "Me four."

"I was ten the first time I caught him," Damon says.

"Hold on. You all knew Dad was cheating on Mom? Why didn't anyone say anything?" I can't believe this. I've been carrying this secret around thinking I was protecting my brothers for nothing?

Brody shrugs. "What was I supposed to say? Hey, Dad, did you screw your secretary? Not the type of breakfast conversation you'd expect in the Bragg household."

"You could have told me." I pat my chest. "Your twin."

"Miller never told me he knew about Dad's indiscretions until we found out about Peace," Elder says.

"I didn't want my brothers to know what a scoundrel our dad was," Damon adds.

Peace collapses on a chair. "You're saying my biological father was a total asshole?"

"Not a total asshole," I say. "He was always there for our baseball games."

"And our school plays," Brody adds.

"And our birthdays," Elder finishes.

"I need to think about this later," Peace says. "Let's discuss what we know about this brother. Or is it a sister?"

"Brother," Elder says. "Dad apparently couldn't make girls."

"What does everyone want to do? Do we contact him?" Peace runs a hand through his hair. "Do I get a vote?" He stands. "Maybe I shouldn't be here."

I place my hand on his shoulder to stop him from fleeing. "You're a Bragg Brother no matter what last name you use. You're welcome here."

My brothers nod in agreement.

"Why don't we sit down and discuss what we're going to do?" I suggest.

Everyone gathers around a table.

"Well," I prod when silence falls. "What are we going to do? Do we approach this guy? Do we ignore him? What?"

Personally, I want to go back to bed and forget this conversation ever happened. I don't need another reminder of my dad's inability to keep it in his pants.

"We're not sure he's Dad's son yet," Elder explains.

"Do you want me to dig into it?" Peace asks.

"I think we should vote on how to proceed first," Damon says.

Brody's eyes widen and his jaw drops open. "Whoa. I must be hearing things." He feigns cleaning out his ear. "Big brother isn't dictating what we do."

"Knock it off. I don't dictate what any of you do."

Brody rolls his eyes at Damon. "You didn't insist I finish the trapeze class?"

"Dude, the class was expensive and you only had one more day left. You were scared and needed a little push. You're welcome."

Peace looks around the table. "I don't know if I should be thankful I grew up as an only child or not."

Elder slaps his back. "You're not an only child now. The question is how many Bragg siblings are there."

"I vote we leave things the way they are," Miller suggests.

Elder rolls his eyes. "Of course, you do. You didn't want to meet Peace."

Miller grunts. "No offense, Peace."

"I get it. No apology necessary."

"I think we should at least find out if this man is actually our brother. Otherwise, we'll always wonder," Damon says. "All in favor?"

"So much for Damon not taking charge," Brody mumbles before raising his hand.

I keep my hands firmly on the table as does Miller.

"Four to two," Damon announces as if the rest of us can't count. "How do we proceed?"

"I can make inquiries," Peace offers.

"That settles it." Damon stands. "Let me know what you find out. I'm out of here."

"Wait. You're not staying in Winter Falls?" I ask.

He shakes his head. "I need to get back."

"What's going on with him?" I ask but everyone's too busy discussing the possibility of us having another brother to pay any attention to me.

I can't discuss it. The possibility of a new sibling reminds me of Dad's inability to be faithful to our mom. Fuck. I thought I'd dealt with all of the backlash from his infidelities.

Crap. What if I am like my dad? I am his carbon copy after all. What if I can't keep my promises to Moon? Is it better if I leave her now? Before I hurt her?

Chapter 28

I was right. You were wrong ~ Text from Moon to Ashlyn

"HI!" I GREET RILEY when I open my door to him. I push up on my tiptoes to kiss him hello. Despite the spark of excitement charging through me, his lips remain immobile. Weird.

"I thought you were coming for dinner. I saved you some."

He stuffs his hands in his pockets and rolls back on his heels. What he doesn't do is look at me. I feel a flicker of fear. I force it away. This is my Riley. Whatever's happening with him, we'll get through it. Assuming there's anything happening. Way to get ahead of yourself, Moon.

I grasp his arm and drag him inside. "Come. Let me warm you up some food."

"I already ate."

Already ate? I'm certain we discussed him coming over to my house for dinner.

"You're acting weird. Is something wrong?"

"We need to talk."

"We need to talk," I mimic in a deep voice. "Sounds serious. Do I need to put on my serious face? I have one around here somewhere."

"It is serious."

I give up on trying to lighten the mood. It's not working anyway. "Uh oh. Is this about what happened with your brothers?"

He frowns. "You already know?"

I spread my arms. "Welcome to Winter Falls."

"How the hell do you know about my new half-brother already? Did one of my brothers tell you? Or are there listening devices planted in the brewery?"

"Whoa. Half-brother? The only thing I know is the Bragg brothers met at the brewery this morning. If anyone knows what was said, they're not talking."

He sighs as he drops his chin to his chest. The flicker of fear in my chest grows to a flame. I ignore it. This isn't about me.

"Let's have a seat and discuss what's happening."

We settle on the couch. I frown when he sits in the corner as far away from me as possible. Not about me, I repeat to myself.

I fiddle with the hem of my sweater while I wait for Riley to begin. I try to wait. I really do. But patience is not a virtue I can claim I possess. Plus, I'm curious. Is there another Bragg brother out there?

"What's this about a new half-brother?"

He runs a hand over his beard. "Another name popped up in the genetic search Miller and Elder did."

Holy shit. How many Bragg brothers are there? I tamp down my curiosity. Riley is obviously not excited about this news.

"What are you going to do?"

"I voted to do nothing."

"But," I prompt when he falls silent once again.

"I got outvoted."

"Which means?" Talking to Riley is more excruciating than laying the tile of the backsplash in the kitchen. I never should have chosen those tiny tiles. What was I thinking?

"Peace is going to research if this *person* could be another one of our siblings." He spits the word person out like it's a nasty word.

Be brave, Moon. Be brave. I squeeze Riley's hand.

"It's not his fault if your dad is his biological father."

"I know. I know. It's just…"

In an effort to give him time to gather his thoughts, I count to thirty. And then I count to sixty. And then I… Screw it.

"It's just what?"

He yanks his hand from mine before jumping to his feet and starting to pace around my living room.

"It's more evidence of my dad being a cheater."

I can't disagree with him there, but I'm afraid he's diving into a deep, dark hole. A hole I thought we agreed to fill with cement and cover up.

"You're not your dad."

"How do I know?" he shouts. "How do I know I'm not a bastard like him? I told you he was a star baseball pitcher in high school like I was, but did I tell you he also dabbled in woodwork?"

"You didn't."

"This is what I mean. I'm him."

I block his path. "No. You are not."

"How do you know? You didn't know him." He snarls.

"No, but I know you." He glares at me, but I'm undeterred. "I know you're not a bastard."

"You can't know that."

I poke his chest. "Yes, I do. I have proof."

"You can't have proof."

"Who stood up for me at the business meeting when the entire town blamed me for the expansion of the brewery? Who helped me with the renovations on the diner during the Christmas break knowing I wouldn't be able to pay him for his time? And who hasn't accepted a dime of my money despite working his ass off for the past month? Who?"

"None of those things proves I'm not going to cheat on you."

I throw my arms in the air. "We've discussed this. Just because your dad was a cheating asshole. Sorry, I didn't mean to call your dad an asshole."

He dismisses my comment with a flick of his hand.

"You're dad being a you-know-what doesn't mean you'll cheat on me."

He steps away from me and I suddenly feel cold. Chilled down to my bones.

"I don't know. Maybe I shouldn't risk it."

The fear I've been pushing away since the moment he arrived at my house rushes through my body at such a speed I nearly fall over.

"You're dumping me."

"I—"

I don't let him finish. "After everything you did to convince me to give you another chance, you're throwing me away."

He grasps my upper arms and shakes me. "I'm not throwing you away. I'm saving you."

I dash at a tear when it escapes. "You're not saving me. You're abandoning me. Just like my parents did."

"No, Moon. I'm not. Don't compare me to them."

I shove my fear and heartache down into the deep hole where they usually live and let the rage take over. Rage is a safer emotion.

"You're a fucking coward."

He flinches and releases my arms. "I'm not a coward. I'm doing what's best for the both of us."

If my eyes were lethal weapons, he'd be a pile of ashes by now. "You're not doing what's best for the both of us. You're running away from your fears. After you made me confront mine, you're running from yours. Hypocrite."

"I'm sorry, Moon. I never meant to hurt you."

"Intentions don't mean a damn thing. Your actions tell me what kind of person you are. And your actions are telling me you're a coward." I step back from him. "I thought you were a better man than this."

"That's what I've been trying to tell you. I'm not."

He heads for the door. I hate myself for it, but I follow him.

"We can figure this out. You don't have to do this."

"Yeah, I do. Goodbye, Moon," he says with his gaze focused on the door handle.

"If you walk out that door, do not come back. Do you hear me? You promised you would love me and you would never leave me. If you break your promise, I don't want to ever see you again."

"I know," he whispers before opening the door and walking right out of my life.

I knew it! I knew I couldn't trust a man. I knew I was better off all on my own. But along comes Riley to convince me otherwise. No more! Moon Star is officially ending her dating days.

I don't need anyone. I can conquer the world all on my own. Screw men and their sweet talking ways and their sexy forearms and their skin that tastes of the sea and sun. It's all a big fat fucking lie.

Chapter 29

I SIGH WHEN THE doorbell rings. I've successfully ignored Ashlyn for an entire day. I guess my time's up. I won't go down without a fight though. Watch me.

"Leave me alone!" I shout in the general direction of the front door.

"The door's locked. Why the hell is the door locked?" Ashlyn grumbles.

Because I'm not an idiot. Because I knew she'd come to check up on me sooner or later. Because I have no intention of being cheered up. You cheer someone up when she lost the best pie competition at the school fair, not when she's heartbroken.

I increase the volume of the television and cuddle deeper into my blanket. She'll go away. Eventually. I hope.

"This is sad," Ashlyn says from where she's now standing at the end of my couch with Harmony and Soleil.

I groan. "How did you get inside?"

She plants her hands on her hips. "You can't keep me out of your house."

Harmony snorts. "She climbed through the window above your sink."

"You should probably get the lock fixed," Soleil adds.

"If you're here to cheer me up, you can turn around and walk right out of here. I'm not in the mood."

Ashlyn rips the blanket off of me and I screech. "What are you doing?"

"Saving you from yourself," she mutters as she grasps my arm and attempts to pull me to my feet.

I bat her away. "Leave me alone."

"Nope. I've left you alone entirely too much."

I frown at her. "What are you talking about? You're practically attached to my hip."

She plops down on the sofa next to me. "Whenever you're hurting, you withdraw and I let you. I shouldn't have."

"You've always been there for me," I insist.

"Not enough." She shakes her finger at me. "No more. I'm not letting you suffer alone anymore. No more holidays spent alone because you claim not to care. No more allowing you to say no to family dinners. I'm done with allowing you to push me away."

I narrow my eyes on her. She's supposed to be bubbly, oblivious Ashlyn. She's not supposed to notice how much I pushed her away.

But it was too painful to be around other happy families when my own family deserted me. At first, it was comforting to have somewhere soft to land. But after it became obvious my parents weren't returning, it just plain hurt.

"I don—"

"Starting now." Typical Ashlyn. Her decision is made and no discussion is allowed. She stands and offers me her hand. "Come on."

I bury my hands under my thighs. "I'm not going anywhere."

Ashlyn is undeterred. She climbs behind me on the sofa and shoves my shoulders. I refuse to budge. "What are you doing?"

"Whatever's necessary."

Those are scary words coming from the prank queen of Winter Falls. I scoot away from her.

"Leave me alone."

She crawls after me. "Not until you agree to attend book club with us."

I freeze. She wants me to leave the house. Is she crazy? Stupid question. It's Ashlyn. Of course, she's crazy.

"I'm not going anywhere." I indicate my outfit of sweatpants with a hole in the thigh and long-sleeved t-shirt with chocolate stains on it.

"You can change," Soleil offers.

"I'm not changing because I'm not going anywhere."

Harmony snorts. "I said the same thing when this one." She points to Ashlyn. "Showed up at my house."

"We can stage a rebellion together," I offer.

"I prefer not to watch Ashlyn burn your house down around us."

She can burn the house down for all I care. It's not as if I enjoy living in the house my parents abandoned me to. But I do need somewhere to live. And I don't have any money to pay rent or a mortgage. Maybe burning the house down is a bit rash after all.

"You have to attend smutty book club," Ashlyn insists. "You promised to make those red velvet chocolate swirled brownies."

"The man I love just walked away from me," I snarl at her. "Did you really expect me to bake?"

I hear a moan from behind me and whirl around. Eden is standing there with a brownie shoved in her mouth. "So good."

"Ha! I knew you'd bake. You always do when you're sad."

I narrow my eyes on her. "Are you saying I'm fat?"

She wags her finger at me. "I'm not falling into your trap." She points to Harmony and Soleil. "You convince her. I have brownies to eat."

While Eden and Ashlyn fight over the brownies, Harmony and Soleil approach me.

"It would do you good to get outside," Soleil says. When Harmony doesn't immediately agree, she elbows her.

"Um, yeah." Harmony's nose scrunches. "It stinks in here."

I lift my t-shirt up and sniff. Oops. I don't think it stinks in here. I think *I* stink.

"I don't want to go," I pout.

Soleil squeezes my hands. "I know. But sitting at home alone isn't going to ease the pain of your heartbreak."

"I hate to admit it. But she's right. Let's go to smutty book club, get drunk, and make ourselves sick by eating a dozen brownies each." Harmony shrugs. "It's basically the same plan you had, but you won't be alone."

"Except I have to share my brownies."

She rolls her eyes. "Tell me you didn't bake six dozen and I'll support staying here."

I made seven dozen but whatever.

"Fine," I huff. "I'll go, but I'm not changing."

When we walk into *Fall Into A Good Book,* the bookstore owned by Ashlyn's sister Aspen fifteen minutes later, I'm wearing a different outfit. I was all set to come in my dirty clothes, but Ashlyn tackled me and started tearing my sweatpants off.

The last thing I needed was for her to see the underwear I was wearing. I'd never hear the end of the teasing about my holey underpants.

"She's here," Sage shouts and rushes toward me with the rest of the gossip gals – Feather, Petal, Cayenne, and Clove – on her heels.

This is why I didn't want to come. I knew the gossip gals would be here. They're always here. Who do you think chooses the smutty books?

Ashlyn shoves me behind her. "No." She wags her finger at Sage. "You won't bother her tonight. Do you understand?"

"But how are we supposed to plan her reconciliation with Riley if we don't speak with her?" Feather pouts.

My hands fist and I growl. "There will be no reconciliation."

I gave him a second chance once. A second chance I didn't want to give him. But he needled and needled his way back into my heart until I couldn't resist him any longer. No more! I am done with him. He is not getting another chance. My heart might not survive this round of heartbreak as it is.

"But Riley's perfect for you," Clove says.

Clementine shoves her way through the gossip gals to stand next to Ashlyn in front of me.

"Enough!" she shouts and my eyes practically bug out of my head. I've never heard Clementine raise her voice before.

"We're not doing anything wrong," Sage says.

Clementine growls at her. She actually freaking growls. "I said enough. You and the rest of your busybody friends have done enough damage here."

"We didn't do any damage," Sage claims.

"I know you know what it's like to be heartbroken," Clementine whispers and Sage's mouth snaps shut.

What's this about? Sage has never been in a relationship before as far as I know. She's been a spinster ever since I can remember.

"Leave my girl out of your matchmaking," Clementine insists. "It's not what she needs right now. What she needs is for you to support her. To sympathize with her. To eat a ton of bad food with her. And definitely to drink too much wine with her."

"I told you we should have hired a stripper," Cayenne mumbles.

"As long as the stripper isn't Miller, I'm in," Eden mutters from next to me.

"You know you want to see him naked," Harmony teases.

"Naked on a slab in the morgue."

Eden could find a reason to bitch about Miller even if the topic is aliens on Mars. One of these days I need to ask her what's going on. Just as soon as I get over this heartbreak. So like in another decade or so.

Clementine stares Sage and her crew down. "Do we have an understanding?"

"But what if—"

"I said," Clementine cuts Feather off. "Do we have an understanding?"

There's a tense moment as Clementine faces off with Sage before Sage nods.

"Good." Clementine motions toward where the drinks and snacks are set up. "Why don't you grab Moon a drink to apologize?"

The gossip gals trudge off with their heads hanging low. My mouth is literally gaping open. I have never – and I've lived in Winter Falls for almost all of my twenty-five years – seen the gossip gals get a dressing down before. Oh, people have tried. Many have tried. They've always lost. Until this moment. Clementine is a dark horse.

"Who's surprised Clementine went all Mama Bear?" Ashlyn asks and I raise my hand.

Clementine's cheeks darken and she wrings her hands in front of her. "I didn't embarrass you, did I?"

I launch myself at her. "Thank you," I whisper as I cling to her. "No one's ever…"

"Shush you. Those days are over," she says as she sways me back and forth.

I feel hands on my back and glance behind me. Eden, Harmony, and Soleil squeeze my shoulders while Ashlyn buries herself around my waist.

I hate to say it. But I think I might have been wrong. Maybe I should have leaned on my friends a bit more instead of withdrawing into myself. Well, today is a new day. I can learn to lean on them without losing my independence. I think.

Chapter 30

RILEY

Something taps my forehead, and I swat it away.

"Get up," Elder orders.

I open my eyes but slam them closed again when the light from a flashlight shines in my face.

"Why are you in my bedroom?"

Instead of answering, he rips the covers off of me.

"Get up now," Brody demands. Great. Elder isn't alone. All of my brothers are probably here in my bedroom. The question is why.

"What are all of you doing here at…" I force my eyes open to check the clock on my nightstand. "Four in the morning?"

"Trust me. I don't want to be here any more than you do. I could be in my warm bed with my woman right now. Instead, I'm here," Peace answers.

"Why are you here?"

Instead of answering, Miller, the largest of all the Bragg brothers, grunts before hauling me out of bed and throwing me over his shoulder.

"If you have a morning boner, I'm going to drop you on your head," he grumbles.

"It's four a.m. My cock is still asleep." As I should be. "I promise I'll go where ever you want me to if you put me down."

"And let you slip away?" Elder shakes his head. "No way."

"It was one time."

"Are you forgetting about the time you jumped off the balcony?"

I kind of was. "Whatever."

Miller drops me on the sofa none too gently. I groan when I notice the shot glasses and whiskey on my coffee table. I should have expected this.

"Are we really doing this?"

"Doing what?" Peace asks.

I motion toward the whiskey. "Truth or punch."

"Don't you mean truth or dare?"

"Nope."

Peace scans the room. "Someone needs to explain."

"When this one," I point to Brody, "got suspended from school for getting into a fight—"

"I didn't fight anyone," Brody insists.

I roll my eyes. "We know. Which is why we tried to get the truth of what happened out of you."

"Except he wasn't talking," Elder says.

"Until I punched him." Miller smiles. "Then, he couldn't talk fast enough."

"So the game is you punch someone until they tell the truth?" Peace asks.

Fuck. I forgot all about this game. We haven't 'played' since we were all in college and coming home for the holidays and summers.

"Yep." Elder nods. "Whoever's in the hot seat." He glares at me. Yeah, yeah, I get it. I'm in the hot seat. "Has to tell the truth or get punched."

"How do you know if they're telling the truth?"

Elder narrows his eyes on me. "We know."

"Okay. What's the whiskey for?" Peace asks.

"A shot for each question," Brody answers.

"So, it's truth or punch or shot?"

"Nope." Brody shakes his head. "Everyone does a shot for each question Riley refuses to answer."

Peace glares at me. "I have a shift in a few hours. You better tell us what crawled up your ass and died before I have to call in sick."

"You already called in sick," Elder says.

"Freedom's taking your shift," Miller adds.

"What?" Peace does not appear happy with this news.

"Freedom's taking your shift," Miller repeats in a loud voice.

"And Olivia knows you won't be home anytime soon," Brody says.

Peace motions toward me. "I'll punch him and he'll tell us the truth. Night over and we can all go back to bed."

"What happened to the peace loving police officer?" I ask.

"He got dragged out of his warm bed," Peace grumbles. "So, I can punch him?"

"That's not how this works. First, we do a shot and then Riley has the opportunity to answer our questions before we punch him," Elder explains as he pours shots.

Miller hands me one and my nose scrunches. "I hate whiskey."

Brody chuckles. "Why do you think we chose it?"

I point at him. "When it's your turn, we're drinking tequila."

He shivers. "Good thing it'll never be my turn."

"I think you mean good thing your brother is a cop."

Peace plants his fists on his hips. "Our relationship will not stop me from throwing your ass in jail if you break the law."

Brody sighs. "He's such a stickler for the rules."

"I'm a police officer. It's what we do."

"Why are you a police officer if you're not going to help your family out in times of crisis?" Brody just can't help himself. He has to push it.

"Crisis. What kind of crisis?"

"A naked man being arrested."

Peace's brow wrinkles in confusion. "Why would I arrest a naked man?"

I laugh. "Because someone," I point to Brody, "always loses his clothes when he drinks tequila."

Peace shrugs. "Winter Falls is okay with nudity. As long as Brody doesn't go running around naked during one of our festivals, there's no reason to arrest him."

I grin. "Oh, running around naked isn't the problem."

"I'm kind of afraid to ask what the actual problem is," Peace mutters.

"The problem is when he drinks tequila, he becomes convinced he's a cat burglar," Elder continues.

"A naked cat burglar," Miller adds.

"Who thinks he can climb through small windows," I finish.

"Hey!" Brody shouts. "I can climb through small windows."

I scratch my chin and pretend to think. "You must have forgotten about the time you got stuck with your head inside the window and your naked ass flapping in the wind."

"The breeze felt nice against my balls."

I glare at him. "But who ended up with your balls in his face?"

"It's not my fault you slipped in the mud and ended up with my junk in your face. You have to admit it's impressive junk." Brody thrusts his hips.

Peace points at Brody. "You are hereby forbidden from drinking tequila within the town limits of Winter Falls."

I sigh. "It's like waving a red flag in front of a bull."

"Sometimes I forget Peace didn't grow up with brothers and then poof!" Elder simulates an explosion with his hands. "He proves me wrong."

"Can we get on with things?" Peace asks. "Some of us have a warm woman in our bed we want to get back to."

Elder lifts his glass. "Truth or punch!"

"Truth or punch," everyone echoes before doing their shot.

The whiskey burns my mouth and doesn't stop burning when it hits my stomach. "Fuck, I hate whiskey."

"Me first," Brody declares.

"I'm the oldest. I get to go first," Elder claims.

Peace clears his throat. "I believe I'm oldest." He glares at me. "What the hell is wrong with you?"

"Lots of things," I answer and hold out my shot for a refill. I may hate whiskey but I know how this game is played. I'm not a cheater. Not when I can't get away with it at least.

Elder elbows Peace. "You have to be more specific. If you ask a broad question, he can give a broad answer without getting punched."

Peace opens his mouth to ask another question, but Elder cuts him off. "My turn. Why did you break up with the woman you love?"

"It wasn't working out," I answer and hold out my glass. The whiskey burns less this time when I drink it.

"He's going to be smashed before we figure out why he's an idiot," Peace grumbles.

"Now, you're getting it." Elder smiles. "Maybe you're starting to understand this brother stuff after all."

Miller studies me before asking, "What reason did you give Moon for breaking up with her?"

Damnit. Miller's too smart for his own good. He also packs a serious punch. This is going to hurt. I stand. "Punch."

"You're seriously going to let Miller punch you instead of answering him?" Peace shakes his head. "Maybe you deserve to be hit."

I stand in the middle of the living room facing Miller. "Hit me with your best shot."

He doesn't hesitate before swinging at my jaw. *Bam!* The force has me falling to the floor. Charlie whines before rushing to me. He stands there barking at Miller until I pet him.

"It's okay, Charlie."

The dog settles down, but he refuses to leave my side as I get to my feet and make my way to the sofa. He leans against my legs and growls at my brothers.

I rub a hand over my jaw. I'm going to have a bruise in the morning. Brody hands me my next shot. I gladly accept it. I hate whiskey but nothing makes the feel of a punch dim as well as a shot of something strong.

"Do you think I would cheat on my girlfriend?" Brody asks.

I snort. "What girlfriend?"

"Answer the question."

"No, I don't think you'd cheat on your metaphorical girlfriend. You're a good guy."

"Then, why do you think you'd cheat on Moon?" he asks.

I scowl. "Party foul. One question per person per round."

Peace doesn't miss a beat. "I hereby grant Brody my question."

I narrow my eyes on him. "You can't grant someone your question. You're breaking the rules."

He crosses his arms over his chest. "We'll make new rules. All in favor of granting someone your turn to pose a question." Miller, Elder, and Brody raise their hands.

"Damon isn't here to vote."

"Doesn't matter. Assuming he agrees with you, the new rule still wins four to two."

I hate how he's right. "Fuck. Fine."

"I'll repeat my question." Brody leans over to get in my face. "If you don't believe I'd ever cheat on a girlfriend, why do you think you'd cheat on Moon?"

"Punch," I say but when I try to stand, I wobble and fall back on the sofa. Shit. How many shots have I had?

"You know the rules. You have to be able to stand for me to punch you."

I glare at my twin. "This is some bullshit."

"You want to hear bullshit? I'll give you some bullshit. You love Moon. You pined for her for months before you came to Winter Falls. Once you arrived, you went balls to the wall to get her to give you a second chance. She finally forgave you and then you go and break her heart because you're a fucking idiot. That's what I call bullshit."

"You don't understand."

"Don't understand? I'm your twin. I understand perfectly."

Peace sits down next to me. "Did you seriously break up with Moon because you're worried you're a cheater the same way your dad was?"

My head falls back against the sofa and I close my eyes before admitting, "Yes."

"Did you fail biology in high school?"

I grunt. "If one more person claims I suck at biology…"

"Do you love Moon?" Elder asks.

I open my eyes to answer. "Yeah."

Love actually sounds too tame a word for how I feel about her. I want to spend every second of every day with her. I want to wake up with her every morning. I want to eat whatever crazy bakery concoction she thinks up next. I want to pretend to understand her jokes even if she's laughing too hard to tell the punchline.

"Then, you need to fix this," Miller insists.

"But—"

"No," Miller growls. "You are not Dad. Did you dip your wick in another woman for the three months you and Moon were apart?"

I rear back. "What? No. I would never."

He points at me. "Exactly. You would never. Our work here is done." He stalks out of the room and out of my house.

My head is swimming. And it's not just from the alcohol. I fucked up. "Shit."

Peace nods. "Shit's right. How the hell are you going to get her back?"

Brody rubs his hands together. "I predict a lot of begging in Riley's future."

I bury my face in my hands. Begging Moon will get me nowhere.

"Don't worry. You've got us. We'll figure this out together," Elder says. "Tomorrow. When you're sober."

"Do we leave him here?" Peace asks.

"It's fine. He's going to pass out any minute."

The last thing I remember is the door shutting behind them.

Chapter 31

I COLLAPSE FACE FIRST on the couch with a groan. Every single muscle in my body hurts – even my pinky finger is sore. I don't know how I'm going to finish the renovations of the diner before Imbolc, which is mere weeks away, but I will.

I don't have a choice. My bank account is now officially blinking bright red with negative numbers. All of the money I made from baking the Hogmanay buns is gone and I don't have any other source of income until the diner opens.

Unfortunately, the diner can't open when the kitchen is a mess. I'd be happy with a cooktop on a camping table at this point, but the health and safety inspectors frown upon that sort of thing. Annoying.

Knock! Knock!

"Go away, Ashlyn."

Knock! Knock!

"I'll call you later. Promise." I'm a liar. I won't be calling her later. She must not agree considering she knocks again two seconds later.

"What's wrong? Your fat ass can't fit through the kitchen window anymore?"

The first thing I did after smutty book club – once I was sober enough to lift a hammer – was fix the window. 'Fix' as in stuck a piece of wood against it to keep it from opening since I don't actually know how to repair a window and the only handyman in town is …

I shut down my train of thought. Riley has been banished from my mind. I might wake up in the middle of the night yearning to be held in his strong arms. Strong arms that make me feel like I belong to someone. Like I'm not alone in this world, but I'll get over it. Eventually.

Knock! Knock!

Ugh. Ashlyn's not giving up. I don't know why I thought she would. The woman doesn't listen to anyone. I don't know how her husband puts up with her.

"Fine. I'm coming."

I roll off the sofa and groan when my sore muscles are forced to catch my weight. My first steps are wobbly, but I eventually make it to the front door.

"You're not Ashlyn," I announce when I open the door to Riley.

He smirks. "I've been accused of a lot of things in my life, but a five-foot-eight blonde woman is not one of them."

His wood and oil scent hits me and I long to wrap my arms around him. But I can't. We're over. *We* will never be anything ever again. I lean against the door and hope I look casual and not like the door is holding me up. Spoiler alert – the door is totally holding me up.

"What do you want?"

"Can I come in?"

I stare at him. Does he seriously think I'm going to let him into my house? Has he gone cuckoo for cocoa puffs?

"What do you want?" I repeat my question instead of yelling at him for thinking he can come into my house. Very adult of me.

He shoves his hands in his pockets. "I want to talk."

I roll my eyes. "Too late."

I gave him the chance to talk to me. I stood right here and begged him not to leave. An action I'm not proud of, but I did it – for him! I would have done anything for him. But he threw me away like I was some stinky trash he couldn't wait to get rid of. I won't let him hurt me again.

"If there's nothing else…" I start to shut the door but he blocks it with his foot.

He clears his throat. "Actually."

I'm such an idiot. "Of course. The money."

I slap myself upside the head. Why else would he be here than to get the money he's owed? He's not here for me. What was I thinking?

"Hold on."

I rush to the kitchen and dig around in the drawer until I find the envelope with the money I owe him. Good thing I didn't spend it. Despite how much of an asshole Riley is, I couldn't use his money for my benefit. It would be wrong.

"Here." I offer Riley the envelope of cash.

"I'm not here for your money."

I roll my eyes. "Of course not. You're here for *your* money." I jiggle the envelope. "Here. Take it."

He rocks back on his heels. "I don't want it."

I slap the envelope against his chest and let go. He's forced to catch it before it falls to the ground.

"I don't want this." He lobs it into my house.

I slap my hand against the door before I slap him. I slapped him once when he returned to town and it didn't make me feel any better. Plus, it's wrong. Violence is wrong. Violence is wrong, I repeat since the temptation to slap him is still awful strong.

"What are you doing? Why are you being difficult? You came here for your money and now you have it."

"This is why I needed the roses."

My nose wrinkles in confusion. "Roses? We don't do cut flowers in Winter Falls."

"I know. Eden gave me a lecture on how they're ruining the environment. I don't understand how she can have a flower shop and not sell flowers."

"*Eden's Garden* isn't a flower shop."

"The lecture kind of clued me in."

I shake my head. The exhaustion is hitting. Exhaustion from working my fingers to the bone. Exhaustion from spending night after night trying to figure out how I'm going to stretch my money to pay my bills. Exhaustion from realizing I will never be with the man I love.

"Why are we discussing flowers?" I ask since I've lost the plot.

"Forget the flowers. I don't care about the flowers. I don't want flowers."

"Okay."

"I want you." He steps forward and I retreat until my back is up against the door. I hold up a hand to stop him.

"We've been down this road before. I'm taking the detour this time. This road is not for me. You're not for me."

"I love you, Moonbeam."

His words slice through me. I've dreamed of hearing those three words spoken by the man I love ever since I can remember. But they don't bring me joy now. I can't trust a man who doesn't have any sticking power. I need a man I can rely on. Someone who shows up even when it's fucking hard.

"Love isn't enough."

I never thought I'd say those words, but it's true. Love can't heal the wounds of being abandoned not once but twice by this man.

"I'll do anything. Tell me what to do and I'll do it."

"Do you have a time machine?"

"Time travel isn't possible."

"Then, you're shit out of luck since you can't travel back in time to when you dumped me for the second time."

Pain flashes in his eyes, but I ignore it. He doesn't have the right to be in pain. I'm the one who was wronged. He's the creator of pain, not the receiver. I am!

"How do I change your mind?"

"What? I'm a woman, so all you have to do is change my mind and all will be okay. Clue in. Nothing is okay!"

Out of the corner of my eye, I notice Feather stop on the sidewalk across the street to eavesdrop on our argument. This is normally the moment I'd drag Riley inside to avoid her overhearing the conversation. Not happening. Let Feather and the rest of the gossip gals blab about my trainwreck of a relationship with Riley. I seriously could not care less. They're going to do what they want anyway.

He drops his chin to his chest. "I know nothing's okay. I can't sleep without you. I can't eat without you. I miss you."

I lean close and hiss at him. "How dare you? How dare you make this about you when you're the one who chose this situation? Not me. I begged you. I freaking begged you to stay and discuss your issues with me and what did you do?" I pause because I deserve to be a drama queen. "You walked out!"

He raises his hands in surrender. "I'm sorry, Moonbeam."

"Stop calling me Moonbeam. I'm not your moonbeam. I'm not your anything. Just leave. You found it easy enough to leave me twice before, so do it again now."

"There's nothing easy about leaving you. You're the love of my life."

"I don't believe you. I'm pretty sure you don't walk away from the love of your life twice."

"I was an idiot."

"Being an idiot isn't an excuse for breaking my heart."

Dang it. I wasn't going to admit to having a broken heart.

"I'm sorry."

He sounds sincere, but if he were sincere, he wouldn't have left me in the first place. He knew if he walked out my door, he wouldn't be welcomed back. He knew! Tears well in my eyes. I need him gone before they spill over. I don't want him to see how he broke me. No one will break me.

"P–p–please." I clear my throat. "Leave."

"There's nothing I can do to change your mind?"

I shake my head. "You have no staying power, Riley."

He steps back and I shut the door.

"This isn't over," he shouts through the door.

"Yes, it is!" I shout back.

I gave him a second chance. He's not getting a third. I swipe at the tears falling down my cheeks. I don't need him. I don't need anyone. I am an island and this island is going to rule the ocean.

Chapter 32

MONDAY

I grunt as I drag the bag of dry mortar across the room. I had to go with buying the bigger bags because they're cheaper, didn't I? These things weigh an absolute ton.

Whoosh! The bag is stolen from my hands. I squeal before I realize who took the bag.

"What are you doing here?" I demand of Riley.

"What does it look like I'm doing?"

Auditioning for sexiest handyman of the year with the bag draped over your shoulder and your arm and chest muscles flexing from the effort? I shake my head. He's a leaver, remember?

"Don't be cute."

He winks. "You think I'm cute."

I growl. "I think you're annoying."

"Are you going to stand around all day and chitter chatter or are you going to help me lay these tiles?"

"I'm laying the tiles," I insist.

And I am. I studied several YouTube videos last night and made copious notes. I can do this.

"Okay. I'll spread the mortar and you can lay the tiles."

He doesn't wait for me to agree on the division of labor before he's pouring the dry mixture into a barrel and adding latex additive to mix it. And now he's switching on the drill making it impossible to have a conversation.

"Chop. Chop," he yells over the sound. "We need to get these tiles laid before the appliances are delivered."

"Whatever," I mutter before stomping outside to bring in the boxes of tiles. I lay them out on the floor and measure the distance from the walls.

"Do you want me to show you how to spread the mortar?" Riley asks.

I want to tell him to take a hike, but I need to know how to do this work because he won't show up every day to help me. Not Riley. Not Mr. Runs At The First Hint Of Fear.

I swallow my growl. "Yes."

He grins. "Grab a trowel."

Tuesday

My knees are aching as I walk into the kitchen of the diner. The last thing I want to do is be on my knees the entire day grouting.

"Don't worry," Riley says from behind me. "The grout is easier to work with." He leans close to study my face. "How is your eye?"

I step back. "It's fine."

It's not. I spent most of the night icing it to dull the pain.

"Here." He offers me safety goggles, a mask, and gloves.

I hold up my hands. "I can't afford those." Those words burn more than the speck of cement dust I got in my eye yesterday. Admitting I'm out of funds literally hurts.

"Don't care. You're using them." He pushes the items into my hands. "Do you think I care about money?"

"Thanks for the reminder." I set the items down on the tile cutter table and remove the envelope from my back pocket. "This is yours."

He growls at me. "If you offer me money one more time, I'm going to put you over my knee and spank you."

A spark of intrigue ignites in my belly and travels down my body until I can feel my core weep at the image of him spanking me. I clear my throat and pray my cheeks aren't red.

"I don't know what the problem is. It's your money."

"Which you can pay me when you're up and running."

"That's not what we agreed to."

Instead of answering me, he walks away. "You want to learn to grout today?"

Damnit. He knows I want to learn to grout. I want to know how to do everything involved in the diner renovations. I will never be beholden to someone else again for doing renovations if I know how to do all of the work myself.

"Let's go."

Wednesday

The backdoor bangs open and Brody saunters inside. "The sexiest man alive is here to help you."

Riley shoves him from behind. "You're a twin. If you're the sexiest man alive, then I am, too."

"Moon can judge." Brody rips off his shirt. "Who's the sexiest man alive? Me or Riley?"

I don't bother studying Brody. His body can't compare to Riley's. I slam my eyes shut to stop visions of Riley's body from dancing through my mind. It doesn't help. All I can see now is his broad shoulders straining as he carries me, his ripped abs as my hands glide over them, and those rough fingertips exploring my body.

"Why the hell is your shirt off?" Miller asks and I open my eyes in time to watch him enter.

Brody waggles his eyebrows. "I'm showing Moon here how she chose the wrong brother."

No reminder necessary. I know I chose the wrong brother. I chose the wrong man period.

Miller slaps him upside the head. "You're a complete idiot."

Elder pushes his way through his brothers. "Why is everyone congregating in the doorway?"

"Um, hello!" I shout to gain their attention. "I think the real question is what the hell are all of the Bragg brothers doing in my kitchen."

Brody puffs up his chest. "We're here for you to use us."

He made things about clear as mud. "Use you?"

"They're going to help me with the delivery of the appliances, cabinets, and countertops," Riley explains.

I hate myself for it, but relief courses through my body. I spent most of last night tossing and turning while trying to figure out how to handle the delivery of the kitchen stoves today.

"You don't have to help," I say despite the relief I feel at their offer of help. "I can—"

Riley growls. "Don't you dare to offer them money for helping."

"Yeah, sis." Brody ruffles my hair. "We're happy to help."

Elder bumps my shoulder. "Family helps family."

Miller grunts. I'm assuming his grunt is his agreement.

I open my mouth intent on explaining how I'm not their family, but Riley places a finger over my lips. The feel of his rough skin doesn't make me shiver. Nope. It's cold in here is all. There isn't any heat on in the place and it's January.

He smiles down at me. "Whether you forgive me and give me another chance doesn't matter. You will always be my family."

His words flow through me leaving fire in their wake. Oh, how I wish I could believe him. I want a family who loves me and who I can depend on. It's the only thing I've ever wanted. But I don't believe him. If he's shown me one thing, it's how I can't depend on him.

"Moon!" Elder shouts to gain my attention. "The delivery truck is here."

I force my gaze away from Riley's ocean blue eyes. "Right. Be right there."

One Week Later

When I arrive at the diner on Monday morning, I'm actually feeling refreshed. At least I think refreshed is what this feeling is. It's been a while since I felt it. With Riley's help last week, I was able to take Sunday off from renovations. My body is thankful.

I smile when I enter the kitchen. It's not quite done yet. I still have to organize all the utensils and pots and pans, but it's nearly there.

I glide my hand along the stainless steel countertops as I make my way to the office. I plan to spend some time on boring administration tasks since I woke up early.

When I open my office door, my eyes widen at the vision I encounter. "What happened here?" I crouch to the floor.

"What are you doing down on the floor?" Riley asks.

"I'm searching for the elves who put the shelves up." I stand and whirl around to face him. "I don't know how they managed to get a new desk and chair in here."

"Does this mean you want me to wear an elf costume?" He waggles his eyebrows. "I'm all in for roleplaying."

"Green tights don't exactly scream sexy."

"I can make anything sexy."

Yes, yes, he can, which is why I'm inching away from him toward the other side of the desk where I can't feel his heat or smell his wood and oil scent. I've never been good at resisting temptation and Riley is one big sexy ball of temptation. Temptation I know will burn me if I touch it.

I gesture to the shelves. "Did you do all of this?" I ask, although I don't know who else could have done the work.

Despite my earlier reference to elves, I'm aware they're not real. I spent enough of my childhood failing in my search for them to know the truth about their existence.

Riley stuffs his hands in his pockets. "You had piles and piles of paperwork everywhere. You needed shelves."

It nearly chokes me, but I swallow my pride. "Thank you."

He smiles and it lights up his blue eyes. Damn it. I need to stop noticing every little nuance in Riley's face. Not healthy.

"You're welcome. But it's up to you to organize everything."

I sigh as I scan the room. This is going to take me all day. I kneel and grab the first pile of paperwork. There's no time like the present to begin.

Tuesday

I rush forward when I spot Riley lifting a toilet out of the bed of his truck.

"What are you doing?" I ask as I try to help him.

"I got it," he grumbles as he carries the toilet toward the rear entrance of the diner. "Can you get the door?"

"Get the door? Why am I getting the door? I didn't order any toilets. I can't afford new toilets." I feel my cheeks heat with the admission. I don't know why. Riley is perfectly aware of my financial situation.

"You better not offer me that envelope of money again."

I might have hidden the envelope in his truck a time or two. It's his money. I'm not going to use it for anything as long as I still owe him, so he might as well have it.

"It's your money!"

"Door," he grunts and I notice his muscles are straining to carry the toilet.

Shit. I rush forward and open the door. He marches straight to the restrooms. I chase after him.

"Stop."

He sets the toilet down and turns to me with his hands on his hips.

"There's nothing wrong with my toilets."

"Yet," he corrects. "There's nothing wrong with them yet. But these toilets are not going to last more than a few years. It makes more sense to replace them now while we're doing renovations than to have to replace them in the future when you're open."

Damnit. He has to be all reasonable! I throw my hands in the air. "Why are you doing all of this? It's not as if you want me back."

Those words burn as I say them.

"Not want you back? How can you possibly think I don't want you back?"

"Because you haven't said anything about wanting another chance."

"Would you give me another chance if I asked?"

I cross my arms over my chest and scowl. "No."

But it'd still be nice if he asked for another chance. Maybe add in a little begging and groveling while he's at it. He places his hands on my cheeks and I let him. Just this once.

"Moonbeam, I know you won't take me back if I beg. Although, if you want me to beg, I can." He waggles his eyebrows and I roll my eyes despite the excitement his words awake in my body. "I know you need to see how you can depend on me. How I won't let you down again."

He drops his hands and steps back. "So, I'm going to show you."

He picks up the toilet and gets back to work while I stand there with my mouth gaping open. Holy crap. He actually listened to me. He understands what I need.

Shit. How am I going to resist him now?

Chapter 33

*R*ILEY

A week has passed since I told Moon I'm going to show her my intention to stick around. I've shown up every single day to help her with the diner. Her eyes have gone from weary to suspicious to intrigued.

I'm not dumb enough to mention the intrigue to her, though. I prefer my balls where they are. Even if I have the worst case of blue balls in history right now.

I glance around the eating area of the diner and sigh. The place is a mess. The walls need to be painted, the booths reattached to the walls, and the counter assembled. And then everything needs to be cleaned before the decorating can begin.

And it all needs to happen – I check my watch – within the next twelve hours since Moon is determined to open in the morning. The Imbolc festival begins tomorrow and tourists are already pouring into Winter Falls.

I won't let Moon down. I know she needs the income from a good weekend to keep her afloat. I don't know how bad her financial situation is, but considering she's tried to skip lunch every day this week, I assume it's bad.

She's crazy if she thinks I'm going to allow her to skip lunch. The same way I won't allow her to pay me. I've told her more times than I can count to keep her money until she's up and running.

But she's stubborn as hell and won't listen. I've found that stupid envelope of cash in my truck, in my jacket, in my mailbox. You name it. I've found the envelope there. She had to tape it together to stop it from falling apart after being bounced around so much.

Which is why I'm standing in front of her office. I wait for her to hang up the phone before I enter and throw the envelope on her desk.

"I thought we agreed to stop doing this shit."

Her eyes narrow on me. "What shit?"

I plant my hands on the desk and lean forward. I don't miss the way her eyes flare and flex my biceps to give her a show. She bites her lip and my cock springs to life.

I swallow my moan. I won't allow Moon to think I want her back for sex no matter how explosive the sex is between us. I want her back for everything. The sex is just a bonus. A spectacular bonus. But a bonus nonetheless.

"You're not paying me until the diner is up and running. We've agreed on this already."

She huffs. "Saying we agree and walking away isn't an actual agreement. Two people have to agree to make an agreement. It's kind of obvious from the word. Agreement. Agree."

"How's this? I'm not accepting the money. I'm insulted you keep attempting to give it to me."

Her nose wrinkles. "Insulted? How have I insulted you?"

"By not accepting my offer of help."

Her nostrils flare and she crosses her arms over her chest. "I don't need your help. I don't need anyone's help."

"It's okay to accept help once in a while." I need to tread cautiously here. Moon doesn't accept help easily. The woman has it in her thick skull that if she accepts help, it means she's not independent. I call bullshit.

"I don't want to depend on anyone."

We've hit the heart of the problem. She doesn't believe she can depend on anyone because her asshole parents abandoned her at a young age. If you ask me, this whole town abandoned her. Instead of drawing her in, they let her go her own way. At least, Clementine has admitted she was wrong and is now Moon's staunchest defendant.

"It's not weak to depend on another person." She frowns. "I depend on my brothers all the time."

"Must be nice," she mumbles.

"You can depend on them, too. One phone call is all it takes and they'll come running."

She shakes her head. "No. I'll finish everything on my own and be open tomorrow."

I rub a hand over my forehead and mumble, "Stubborn."

She scowls. "What did you say?"

"Nothing. Let's go. The walls aren't going to paint themselves."

I can't help but notice the groan she lets out as she slowly stands. Her muscles have to be aching after the past three weeks of going balls to the wall to get this place finished up in time for the festival. I should know. My muscles are feeling the strain, too, and I'm used to doing manual labor.

I don't remark on how slowly she's moving and make my way to the front of the diner where I have the supplies all ready to paint.

"Can you tape off the windows and I'll get the paint gun going?"

"Got it."

I should be paying attention to what I'm doing, but I can't keep my eyes off of Moon. She's wearing a pair of overalls with the top tied around her waist allowing me a view of her perfect breasts in her tight t-shirt.

"Ahem. See something you like?"

I smirk. "I don't know. Maybe I need a closer look."

She rolls her eyes. "Fat chance, buster."

I shrug. "It was worth a try."

I return my attention to the walls before she notices the smile on my face. Progress. Flirting is definitely a step in the right direction, but I'm still cautious. Moon is skittish. Which is entirely my fault.

Once the painting is finished, we begin construction of the counter while the walls dry.

"Can you grab my hammer?" I ask Moon. "I left it on the kitchen counter."

She points to my hand. "You're holding a hammer."

"This is a mallet, not a hammer."

"Whatever," she mumbles before leaving to find my hammer.

Five minutes later, I realize she hasn't returned. I better go help her.

"Did you not…" My words trail off when I discover Moon fast asleep in the kitchen with her torso draped over the counter.

She doesn't stir when I pick her up. I set her down on her chair in her office. I'd rather she went home, but there's no way I'm waking her to say anything of the sort. As soon as she's awake, she'll be working again. Maybe this way she can get a few hours of sleep.

I'm already fishing my phone out of my pocket to call my brothers before I shut the door behind me. I wanted to bring them in to help earlier, but Moon wouldn't hear of it. She can't complain when she's asleep, though.

Brody arrives first. He studies the area before sighing. "I'm glad I don't have a date tonight."

Miller and Elder arrive next. "What do you need us for?"

I motion toward the room. "We're opening tomorrow."

Elder's eyes widen. "Shit. We better get to work."

My brothers may be assholes who make me drink whiskey and punch me when I won't tell them my secrets, but they don't hesitate to help when I need them. Actually, it's Moon who needs them. I wish she could understand how much support she has. All she has to do is ask for it.

I force those thoughts away. Work now. Convince Moon to fall back in love with me later.

"What's going on in here?"

Moon's shout wakes me and I tumble from the chair I was sleeping on to the floor. She giggles and it's the sweetest sound in the world. I hope we have daughters who giggle the way she does.

I push to my feet and stretch out my aching muscles. "Do you like it?"

Her eyes flare as she stares at the strip of skin exposed from where my t-shirt hikes up when I stretch. I prolong my stretch to give her a good view. She deserves something pretty to look at and I'm happy to oblige.

"Y-y-es," she stutters.

I know she's not talking about the dining area. "You like the room?"

She clears her throat and forces her gaze away from me to study the room. "How did this happen?" Her gaze lands on the clock. "Shit. It's nearly six in the morning. We have a ton of stuff we need to finish before we can open."

Her hands flail in the air and I grasp them. "Whoa. It's okay, Moon. Everything's ready."

"Everything? What about the little stuff? Napkin dispensers on every table. Salt and pepper on every table. The menus. The—"

I place a finger on her mouth to quiet her before she starts hyperventilating. "All done."

I wrap an arm around her shoulders and haul her near before brandishing my arm toward all the tables. "Miller and Elder helped."

"Hey." Brody's head pops up from one of the booths. "I helped, too."

"Don't forget me," Peace adds.

Her eyes widen as she notices we're not alone. "Are there Bragg brothers sleeping on every bench in my diner?"

"I'm technically not a Bragg brother," Peace points out as he stands. "I need to get home. I have another shift today." He salutes as he exits the diner.

"Thank you!" Moon shouts after him.

"You can thank me with a kiss." Brody taps his cheek and Moon giggles as she pushes up on her toes to kiss him. I growl at my brother and he smirks before following Peace out the door.

Miller groans as he stands. He kicks Elder's feet.

"Knock it off," Elder grumbles as he rises.

Miller wipes a hand down his face. "Need to get to the brewery."

"Thanks for helping out," Moon says and he grunts in response.

Elder waves as he follows his twin out the door.

Moon looks up at me. "I can't believe you did all of this."

I cradle her face with my hands. "Of course, I did all of this. I wasn't going to let you down again. I'm never letting you down again."

There's a storm in her eyes as she contemplates my words. She opens her mouth to speak but before she gets the chance, the rear door bangs open.

"I'm here boss," Eagle hollers as he walks in.

Moon blinks and steps away. Damn. I was sure she was about to forgive me and give me another chance. I shake my head. Today is not about me. Today is about the launch of Moon's Diner.

"I need to…" She waves in the general direction of the kitchen.

"Go," I urge. "I'll double check everything is ready for your big opening."

Her smile is bright enough to light the winter sky. "Thank you," she whispers and bounces away.

Chapter 34

THE MORNING FLIES BY. It's not the grand opening of *Moon's Diner* I had envisioned – with special opening pastries, decorations, and a signature drink to celebrate. I'm just happy to hear the ca-ching of the cash register. Although happy isn't quite right. I'm ecstatic. My cheeks hurt from how much I'm smiling.

"Get out of here. I've got everything handled," Eagle says as he shoos me out of the kitchen. Again.

"I want everything to be perfect."

He places his hands on my shoulders. "Darling, nothing in life is perfect. It's messy and complicated and full of twists and turns. Enjoy the ride."

"Why are we discussing life? Are you giving me life lessons now?"

He steps away with a shrug. "Someone has to before…" He clears his throat and cuts himself off.

I narrow my eyes on him. "You're lucky I'm too busy to interrogate you."

"You're welcome to try," he says with a wink before returning his attention to the eggs he's frying.

"Moon pie!"

I enter the dining room and search the area for my best friend who's in a stare down with Harmony.

"What's happening, Ashlyn Bashlyn?"

Ashlyn points at Harmony. "Your waitress claims you don't have any red velvet chocolate swirled brownies. I've been looking forward to them all morning." She sticks out her bottom lip and pouts.

Ashlyn's daughter, Patience, sensing her mom's distress lets out a wail. I steal the baby and set her on my hip.

"Hi, baby girl. Is your mommy being difficult?"

"I'm not difficult," Ashlyn claims.

"She's lying, isn't she?" I coo to the baby.

I sense someone's eyes on me and scan the crowd until my gaze catches on Riley. His eyes are tender as he watches me holding the baby.

"Yoowza!" Ashlyn shouts. "Someone wants to make a baby with Moon."

I swear Riley mouths *I do.* I blink my eyes. The lack of sleep must be causing me to hallucinate. Riley doesn't want to have a baby with me. Or, maybe he does, but he can't be trusted. He doesn't have any staying power.

Which is why he spent the past month working every single day at the diner for you for free, a little voice in my head whispers. I tell her to shut up. Naturally, she doesn't listen. *You know you're ready to forgive him. You almost did this morning. But you're a chicken.*

I force those thoughts out of my mind and face Ashlyn. "Sorry. I didn't have time to make any brownies."

She waggles her eyebrows. "Because you were too busy buttering Riley's buns?"

Harmony giggles. "Leave it to Ashlyn." A customer calls her away and she rushes off.

"I should get back to work. Do you want to order anything?"

"The morning special to go, please. Rowan's been hankering for Eagle's pancakes."

I hand Patience back to Ashlyn before going to place her order. I notice a line at the cash register and hurry over there.

"Can you give Harmony her tip for me?" Forest asks as he offers me a ten dollar bill.

"You can put it in the tip jar. We divide the tips at the end of the day."

I indicate the jar and my eyes nearly pop out of my head when I notice what's in there. The envelope. I'm going to kill Riley. Kill him dead. I somehow manage to keep a smile on my face as I finish helping the customers in the line.

"Riley!" I shout the second the last person in line exits the diner.

He pauses with bussing the tables and glances over his shoulder at me. I wave the envelope in the air. He mumbles a curse under his breath before setting the tub on the table and walking toward me with his hands in the air.

"Don't you dare throw that envelope at me," he growls.

Who does he think he is? How dare he sound angry? I'm the injured party in this scenario.

The bell over the door chimes as Sage and her gossip gal gang rush inside.

"This is going to be good." Sage is practically drooling.

"This passion must be explosive in bed," Feather adds.

"If you're coming in the diner, you need to order," I demand.

They hurry to sit around a table in the middle of the room.

"Harmony will be right with you," I tell them in a saccharine sweet voice before I snatch Riley's hand and drag him to my office.

"No fair," Sage calls after us, but I ignore her. Despite what she thinks, my job in life is not to entertain her.

I slam the office door behind me before I whirl around to confront Riley.

I slap the envelope on his chest but he doesn't move to take it. "This is your money."

He nods. "It is."

I smile. Finally! We're getting somewhere.

"I accepted it and then I spent it."

I wag my finger at him. "You didn't spend it. You gave it right back to me."

"Am I or am I not allowed to do whatever I want with *my* money?"

I narrow my eyes on him. This is a trick question if ever I heard one before.

He cups my face with his hands and I bite my tongue before I lick his hands. How does he smell this good after working all night and bussing tables all morning? Granted. He went home to shower and change, but he wasn't gone more than fifteen minutes.

"I don't want to be your handyman."

I frown. "But I hired you as my handyman."

"I want to be the boyfriend who helped you get your business up and running."

Damnit. When he peers at me with those ocean blue eyes, it's impossible to say no to him. Especially when I can feel his rough fingers gliding along the skin of my neck and smell his wood and oil scent.

Kiss him. You know you want to. It's not the little voice in my head urging me on this time. It's just me. I want him. I blow out a breath as a weight lifts from my shoulders at the admission. I never stopped loving him.

"I want that, too," I admit, and happiness sparkles in his eyes. "But I can't trust you."

The happiness turns to determination as he nods. "Okay. I'll keep working on gaining your trust. I figure I might win it back in time for us to spend some quality time on the porch in our rocking chairs when we're in our eighties."

"You would—"

My question is cut off when Sage yells my name.

"I'll be right with you," I shout back.

"You need to come now." Her words are accompanied by a knock on the door.

I close my eyes and sigh. "Sometimes Winter Falls drives me crazy."

Riley chuckles. "I love it."

I cock my head and stare at him. "You're serious?"

He kisses my nose. "It's a good thing I'm serious because I'm not leaving Winter Falls unless you do."

"Are you sure you're not the one who got dropped on his head as a baby?"

The door flies open. "None of my boys got dropped on their heads as babies."

"Mom," Riley greets the woman with a kiss before throwing his arm over her shoulders and hauling her closer to me. "Moon Star, please meet my mother, Daisy Bragg."

I hold out my hand. "It's nice to meet you."

She shoves my hand out of the way and enfolds me in her arms. "Family hugs," she murmurs before letting me go.

She holds onto my forearms as she studies me. "I can see why you love her, my boy. She's a stunner."

I feel my cheeks warm.

"And she can cook and bake," Riley adds.

His mom giggles. "This is your diner?"

Pride rushes through me. "Yep. We opened today."

"I can't wait to eat here."

"Let's get you a table."

She waves me off. "I'm not in a hurry. I have plenty of time."

Plenty of time? "How long are you staying in town?"

She smiles and I realize she's beautiful. Considering how gorgeous her sons are, I'm not surprised she's a beauty. "Oh, I'm not leaving. I'm moving to Winter Falls."

"You are?" This is news to me.

"Riley said he wants me to be here to support you."

My eyes nearly pop out of my head at her announcement. Here to support me? I don't know this woman. Why would she move to Winter Falls to support me?

Riley groans. "Mom."

"What?" She widens her eyes as if she's clueless as to what she's doing, but I notice the sparkle in them. She's not innocent. She's a troublemaker. I think I may like her.

"You weren't supposed to tell her," Riley grumbles.

"What was I supposed to tell her?" His mom is good at the innocent act. I should make notes.

"You're moving to Winter Falls because your sons are here."

She frowns. "They are, but I'm not moving here to be close to them. I'm moving here because you need me to support you and your girlfriend. You were quite clear about this on the phone."

"Hold on," I interrupt because I need all the details. "What did he tell you?"

Riley stands in front of his mom. "Nothing."

She peeks out from behind his back. "He told me plenty." She winks. "He thinks you need more people to support you and asked if I'd be interested in the job. I've never had a daughter before, so I packed up my things and here I am."

"A d-d-daughter?"

"This is why you weren't supposed to tell her." Riley runs his hands through his hair. "She's going to freak out and I'm going to have to start all over again. I need to ease her into the idea of having support. She's not used to people being there for her."

I launch myself at him. "Thank you." I bury my face in his chest while I wrangle with the tears welling in my eyes. When I manage the feat, I glance up to discover we're alone in my office with the door closed.

Riley sits in the office chair with me in his lap. I scramble to stand but his hands dig into my waist. "Not ready to let you go."

"You're not letting me go. I won't let you. I'll fight you tooth and nail if you pull another leaving me stunt. But I am worried the chair will collapse under our weight."

He smirks. "Don't worry. I made sure it was extra strong when I bought it."

I glare at him. "Awful sure of yourself, weren't you?"

The humor in his face vanishes. "No, Moon, I wasn't. The only thing I was sure of was that I wasn't giving up."

"You're that certain of me?"

He palms my neck and drags me forward until our foreheads are touching. "I've never been more certain of anything in my life. I know I screwed up and I'm willing to wait for as long as you need me to."

I make the decision I never thought I'd make. "There's no reason to wait anymore."

Hope flares in his eyes. "No?"

"I can't resist you anymore. I don't know what you're going to do next. Fly me to the moon? I can't chance it. Do you know how bad space travel is for the environment?"

"I guess you're going to have to give me another chance or we're going to the moon."

"I don't need grand gestures."

"Trust me, I know. If it were up to my brothers, there would have been a giant inflatable cookie asking you to give me another chance."

"A giant inflatable cookie?"

"Don't ask."

I inhale a deep breath and take a giant leap. "I love you, Riley Bragg."

His smile stretches from ear to ear. "And I love you, Moonbeam. I have from the moment I met you and you schooled me on how I was eating my lunch."

My nose wrinkles. "Steak should never be eaten well done. It's sacrilege."

"If I promise to never order a well done steak again, will you give me another chance?"

I pretend to consider it. "No well done hamburgers either."

"Done!"

His mouth crashes down on mine. I sigh and his tongue thrusts forward. I moan as his taste hits me. I've missed this. I've missed him. No more. I'm never letting him go.

"You asshole!" Eden shouts and I wrench my lips from Riley's with a groan.

"We better go check on what's happening."

"I'm not an asshole!" Miller shouts back.

Riley sighs. "Welcome to the family."

"Thank you for giving me a family."

"I plan to give you everything you've ever wanted."

Chapter 35

EDEN

"Welcome to *Eden's Garden,*" I greet the tourists as they enter my store.

"*Eden's Garden,*" the man snickers.

I keep my smile firmly affixed on my face. I'm used to tourists making fun of my name and the name of my store. Yes, my name is Eden. And, yes, I own a plant store named after the biblical paradise.

But it's not like I'm going to kick anyone out for laughing at my name or the store's name. I can't. I need the business the tourists bring to keep my store afloat. Although, I'm barely afloat. More like bobbing up and down in the waves of the ocean hoping someone will throw me a lifeline.

"Can I help you?"

"I want to buy my girlfriend a bouquet of flowers," the man says.

I lock my body before I cringe. I don't sell bouquets of flowers. I don't sell cut flowers at all. Cut flowers are not sustainable and are therefore not welcome in Winter Falls. I don't explain all of this to the tourists, though. They don't care what *Imbolc* – the festival we're celebrating today – means. They're here for fun, nothing more.

"Can I interest you in a potted plant?" I motion to the display at the window. "I have some lovely violets."

The woman's nose wrinkles. "I don't want a plant. I don't have a green thumb."

I hate the whole green thumb thing. It's a total misconception. There aren't some people who were born better able to care for plants while others kill plants by merely looking at them. How ridiculous.

"There are care instructions included with the pot and plant," I say instead of giving her a lecture about plant care. Been there. Done that. Never ends in a sale. The saying the customer's always right should really be the customer is always right if you want to make money.

The woman grabs the man's hand and leads him toward the door. "Let's look around the town. Maybe there's another *better* gift you can buy me."

I don't miss the emphasis on better. Such a nice lady. Not.

"Have a blessed Imbolc," I call as they leave.

Soleil enters as they exit. "Hey, Eden," she greets. "You ready to go to the diner?"

I sigh. "Yeah."

All ready. No need to lock up and worry about whatever money's in the cash register since there's none in there. I haven't made one sale yet today. Mean girl and her boyfriend aren't the only tourists who aren't interested in my potted plants.

"What's wrong?" Soleil asks.

I force a smile on my face. "Nothing. Why?"

"You look constipated."

I snort. "Um, thanks?"

"Come on." She bumps my shoulder. "Tell Soleil what's wrong."

"I haven't made any sales this morning."

She frowns. "You haven't? But you're using my pots."

I roll my eyes. "The plant is supposed to be the attraction, not the pot."

Although, her pots are gorgeous since Soleil is an artist. She dabbles in many things – including knitting vibrator covers – but her pottery is her biggest success.

"I don't get how my pots without plants sell better than yours with the plants. My pots are literally made for your plants."

She's not exaggerating. We work together on the colors and shapes of the pots best suited to whatever plants are in season and then she makes the pots. It's a great working relationship – assuming I could actually manage to sell some plants.

"Maybe you should sell the pots without the plants," Soleil suggests.

I shake my head. "I'm not taking a cut of your profit."

She checks her watch. "This is an argument for another day. I don't have much time to congratulate Moon on her opening today. I have a pottery class starting in less than an hour. Let's go."

I'm not ready to give up on the argument. "But…"

The words die on my lips as I catch Miller marching past on the sidewalk. I don't think so. Without realizing my feet are moving, I follow. This is all his fault. Him and the stupid brewery expansion. He couldn't let it go?

Between the restaurant and the beer, the brewery makes plenty of money as it is. Why do they need more when some people are barely scraping by? I think of the empty cash register. Not even scraping by.

"Hey!" I holler at him but with the crowds of the festival, he doesn't hear me. There's also a possibility he's ignoring me. I wouldn't put it past him. The man hates me.

I rush after him.

"Is this a race?" Soleil asks as she chases after me.

I'm too busy seething to respond to her. All of my problems – every single one of them – are Miller's fault. My business is failing because of him. I'm done with him denying it. Today is the day he admits what an absolute asshole he is.

I follow him into the diner where he's greeting Harmony with a hug. He twirls her around as she giggles. A ball of something ugly forms in my stomach. And, no, it's not jealousy. I am not jealous of my friend.

What's there to be jealous of anyway? I don't want Miller. I don't care how gorgeous he is with thick, brown hair and warm brown eyes. He's a jerk who's ruining my life.

I stomp toward them. "I hope you're happy with yourself."

"Uh-oh," Harmony mumbles before pushing away from Miller and moving to stand next to Soleil.

Miller frowns down at me. Considering our height difference, he has to look way down. Which only serves to piss me off more. I hate being the short one.

"You're ruining my life."

"You're doing a damn good job of ruining your life on your own, flower girl."

"Don't call me flower girl."

"What do you want me to call you? Flower child?"

"You asshole!"

"I'm not an asshole!"

"An asshole is an irritating person. You are irritating." I poke his chest. Ow! It's hard as granite. "Therefore, you're an asshole."

"I'm tired of you blaming me for all of your problems. It's not my fault the town agreed to the expansion of the brewery."

I throw my arms in the air. "Of course, it's your fault. There wouldn't be an expansion of the brewery if you didn't apply for it."

He crosses his arms over his chest and my eyes do not drop to follow how his biceps flex with the movement. They don't!

"What is your problem with the expansion? It doesn't encroach on your land."

"I've told you this a dozen times before. Do you have memory problems?"

Brody pops up behind him. "He was dropped on his head as a child."

A woman sighs. "No son of mine was dropped on their head."

Crap. Is this the mother of the Bragg brothers? Poor woman. Raising five hellions must not have been easy. Do I introduce myself? Probably not the best time considering I'm yelling at her son, but it's not my fault her son is an asshole.

"We came here for Project Do Over, but the way things are going, we need to start Project Enemy," Sage comments.

I point at her. "There will be no matchmaking. Do you understand? I will not be a pawn in your game."

"But will you be a pawn in Miller's game?" Feather asks and my head nearly explodes.

I ignore her. I can't with the gossip gals today. I just can't. They're crazy and annoying and interfering on the best of days. And today is not the best of days.

I return my attention to Miller. "The expansion will create a shadow on my field."

He scratches his beard. "Not all plants need sun. Maybe you can maneuver your garden around."

"Maneuver my garden around? Have you lost what's left of your mind?"

He shrugs. "I don't understand what the big deal is."

"You wouldn't," I grumble.

"Um, Eden." Moon approaches. "While I appreciate the show you're giving my customers, I think it might be time to take this conversation somewhere else." She thumbs her finger toward the gossip gals. "Somewhere private."

"No need. There's no talking with this Neanderthal," I say and stomp to the door. I stop with my hand on the doorknob.

"Congrats on your opening," I holler because I may be spitting mad but I'm not a bitch who's going to forget to acknowledge her friend achieving all of her dreams.

Riley wraps his arms around Moon's waist and props his chin on her shoulder. Apparently, my friend has achieved more than her dreams today. Good for her. My eyes shift to Miller. Knock it off, eyes. I don't long for him.

"Thank you." She smiles and waves me off. She knows I can't be in the same room as Miller. Hell, everyone in town knows.

I scowl at Miller one more time before opening the door and marching away.

Chapter 36

TWO MONTHS LATER

My feet are dragging and my eyes are barely open as I trudge up my porch to the front door. Business at the diner is hopping. I need to hire more personnel soon. But I'm waiting until I have a bit more money in my reserves before I do.

In the meantime, I'm working twelve-hour days during which I'm constantly on my feet and then, in the evenings, I can enjoy my free time by doing the necessary administrative tasks for the diner. Being my own boss is a ton of work.

Don't get me wrong. I wouldn't change it for the world. But I'm dead on my feet.

I twist the handle but the door doesn't open. Freaking Riley strikes again. He insists I lock my door, despite no one else in Winter Falls locking their door. Locking your door is for when you're hiding. Or having sex if you manage to remember before clothes come off.

"Riley," I shout, but I already know it's useless. The house is dark.

I pat my front pockets. No house key. Because Riley – interfering once again – won't let me keep my house key on the same keychain as the diner keys. It's unsafe for reasons I cannot fathom to understand.

I'm too tired to deal with this. Maybe I'll curl up and sleep on the porch swing. If a cold front hadn't come through today, bringing temps in March down to around freezing, I'd be tempted.

I dump the contents of my bag on the mat in front of the door. Packets of gum, my sunglasses, my wallet, and a ton of receipts tumble to the ground but no key. I shake the bag and hear a jingle. Aha! The key must be at the bottom.

But when I try to put my key in the lock, it won't fit. I turn the key upside down. Still doesn't fit. I squint at it but it's the same damn key with the smiley face keychain I've been carrying around with me since first grade.

I dig my phone out of my pocket and phone Riley.

"Hey, Moonbeam."

Despite how tired I am and how annoyed with him I am, my body warms at his nickname for me. I hope it always does.

"Hey, handyman."

He chuckles. "What do you need?"

"My key doesn't work," I whine.

"Is it the correct key?"

"Yes," I huff. "I think I know what the key to the house I've been living in my entire life looks like."

"Okay. Okay. I have a key to your house. You can come over here and pick it up."

"Do I have to? I'm tired. I just want a hot bath and to fall into bed." I realize I sound like a whiney teenager, but I can't help it. I'm seriously on my last fumes here.

"Sorry, Moonbeam. I'm in the middle of staining a piece. If I stop now, there will be streaks and I'll have to start all over."

"I hate how you have a good excuse."

He chuckles. "It's a two-minute walk. Come on. You can do this." He lowers his voice. "I'll make it worth your while."

My body, which was ready to curl up on the porch and fall asleep two minutes ago, wakes up. It's on board with this plan.

"See you soon," I say and hang up.

I reach Riley's house in less than two minutes. What can I say? My body is ready to be spoiled by Riley. He does the best spoiling. The man works with his hands and knows how to use them.

I frown when I notice the garage is dark. Shouldn't Riley be in there now staining some wood or whatever it is he does in there?

The porch light switches on and Riley steps out. I smile and rush up the stairs before launching myself at him. He twirls me around before touching his lips to mine. I pout when he pulls away.

"More," I insist.

"Don't worry." He winks. "You'll get a whole lot more. But first."

He hands me an envelope. I frown. "Is this …"

The envelope is worn and barely held together with tape. Just like the envelope of money Riley refused to accept for his work.

"I thought we solved the whole money issue?"

He nudges the envelope. "Open it."

"Okay." I open it to discover a key inside. "This is your key to my house. Why are you giving me your key in an envelope?"

He shrugs. "Maybe it's not my key to your house. Maybe it's *your* key to *our* house."

I narrow my eyes at him. "Is this your way of asking me to move in with you?"

We've discussed moving in together, but I've been too tired to consider it. And, okay, maybe I wanted to wait a while to make sure Riley isn't going anywhere. Can you blame me?

He opens the door behind him. "Surprise."

"Surprise? What surprise?"

I follow him inside. Candles are set up on every available surface. "What's going on?"

"Don't you notice anything different?"

"You mean besides the candles and … is that champagne?"

"Yes." He grasps my hips and twirls me until I'm facing the sofa. "Notice anything different now?"

"Hold on. This is my sofa. And my throw pillows. And my blankets. What's going on?"

"My brothers and I moved your stuff to my house today while you were working."

"What? You couldn't ask me?"

He tucks a strand of hair behind my ear. "Moonbeam, I did ask. You said as soon as you had some free time to move, we'd move in together."

"I did?" Oh shit. I did. I didn't realize he'd take my words as an okay to go ahead and move my stuff into his place.

"But we never discussed where we would live."

He palms my neck and leans his forehead against mine. "Moonbeam, we were never going to live in your house."

I slap his chest. "What's wrong with my house?"

"You hate it there. It's your parent's house and every time you walk in there your nose wrinkles like you're smelling something bad."

"I didn't think you noticed."

He kisses my nose. "I notice everything about you. I love you."

I let those words settle into my soul before nodding. "You're right. I don't want to live in that house anymore. I didn't realize I had a choice."

"And?" he prompts.

"And what?"

"You l-l-lov…"

I giggle. "I love you, handyman. To the moon and back."

His eyes light up. "Is the trip to the moon back on?"

"You're crazy."

Woof!

"What's wrong with Charlie?"

He grins. "Time for part two of your surprise."

"There's a part two?"

He leads me to the kitchen where Charlie is barking at a box on the floor. I kneel down next to him. "What's wrong, Charlie? Is it food?"

"Open it," Riley says.

I dive at the present. I don't bother untying the bright red ribbon. I fling it off before opening the flaps.

"You didn't?" I squeal when I see what's inside.

"Go on. Take her out."

I wrap my hands around the furry ball and sit back on my haunches to cuddle her.

"Is she mine?"

Riley sits on the floor next to me. "She's ours."

I smile over at him. "I like the sound of that."

"Good, because you're going to be hearing it for the rest of our lives."

"Love you," I say before kissing him. It's a brief kiss. I have a wiggling bundle of fur in my arms to deal with. "Do you need some loving, too?" I ask the dog and she yips as she tries to climb and reach my face. I hold her away from me.

"What are we going to name her?"

I consider Riley's question. "How about Blondie?" I scratch her behind the ears. "What do you think, girl? Does Blondie sound like a good name to you?" She yips. "There you have it. Her name is Blondie."

Charlie howls before laying his head in Riley's lap. "Are you feeling left out?" I ask and place Blondie in front of him. He sniffs her once before licking her ear.

"Love at first sight," I declare.

"Fitting since I fell in love with you at first sight," Riley says.

"And I, despite your horrid taste in steak, fell in love with you at first sight, too."

I feel something wet on my leg and glance down to find Blondie peeing on me.

"I guess that's one way to bless our moving in together."

D. E. Haggerty
Love and Laughter in Every Chapter

About the Author

D.E. Haggerty is an American who has spent the majority of her adult life abroad. She has lived in Istanbul, various places throughout Germany, and currently finds herself in The Hague. She has been a military policewoman, a lawyer, a B&B owner/operator and now a writer.